Joined at the Heart

Joined at the Heart

Nance Vizedom

Northwest Publishing Inc.
Salt Lake City, Utah

Joined At The Heart

Portions of this story were inspired by events
based on the recollections of the character Anne Edwards-Blake.
Composite characters were used. Fictional events, names, locations and
identifying information were added for individual anonymity.

For information address: Northwest Publishing, Inc.
6906 South 300 West, Salt Lake City, Utah 84047
JAC 2.22.94

PRINTING HISTORY
First Printing 1994

ISBN: 1-56901-232-6

NPI books are published by Northwest Publishing, Incorporated,
6906 South 300 West, Salt Lake City, Utah 84047.
The name "NPI" and the "NPI" logo are trademarks belonging to
Northwest Publishing, Incorporated.

PRINTED IN THE UNITED STATES OF AMERICA.
10 9 8 7 6 5 4 3 2 1

To my loving family—with all my love
and for you, Bobby.
God Bless your mother and sister.
A heartfelt thanks to my friends and loved ones for your support and encouragement.

Prologue

1992—AUSTIN

Feeling strangely detached, Anne scanned the faces seated before her. A grasping ache spread and tightened its claws forcefully around her forehead. She clenched the Eulogy. She feared the slightest movement would set off an avalanche inside her throbbing temples. Struggling to focus on her friends and family, she forced herself to resist the current tugging her thoughts to the past.

For a moment, she drew strength through her husband's blue, gentle eyes. She hoped he sensed her gratitude for his love and support through this time. Her eyes traveled across the room then rested on her daughter. Thick fringes of curled lashes framed her dark, delicately almond-shaped, eyes. Vanessa reflected a compassionate, steady gaze offering support and encouragement to her mother. God, how I love you, Anne thought. Feeling the bond between them strengthen, Anne's eyes flickered with pride at the young beautiful woman her little girl so quickly grew to be.

Thick, heavy air hovered as pain slammed through her in icy waves. With determined effort, she drew in her breath darting her eyes from one face to another.

Maggie, one of her dearest friends, sat in the second row beside her aunt and uncle. Anne's sister, Nina, sat motionless beside their brother, Robert. Watery gray tones of grief tinted her milk white complexion, and Robert's jaw tightened as he tried to keep composure painted on his strong, angular face.

A fistful of needles jamming into the base of her spine jolted Anne back to the letter she needed to read for the eulogy. She lowered her eyes, stared emptily at the printed words, and fought the fragmented memories exploding in her mind. She opened her mouth, but her heart slithered up into her throat.

Anne winced at the uncanny way funerals have of tearing down façades and putting in perspective what life and death are all about. She stood there, now, with raw open wounds exposed to everyone. She felt vulnerable and empty. She grieved to think of her actions, no matter what the cause, and how they contributed to this untimely death. This cruel twist of fate yanked her worst nightmares into bitter reality.

Dark circles of pain framed her tired eyes, and a hint of gray hair conspicuously tapering her delicate face fell forward. She threw her hand up to brush away the smeared liquid oozing down her cheeks. With final determination, she then took a deep breath focusing only on the words before her.

Softly she breathed the words in her letter somehow hoping they would answer his haunting questions. The words trembling from her lips reflected the fundamental agony of her childhood. They were brimmed with pathetic excuses of her actions. Vague recollections of the past she so tightly kept closed in a secret part of her started to gush forth with amazing, sickening clarity.

Chapter One

PITTSBURGH, PA.—1968

"Hey, it's a mighty long walk home," Evan playfully taunted as he eyed Anne's full figure. Her chestnut hair gleamed reflecting the light flickering gently through gaps in the clouds. It was a crisp, autumn day full of sunshine and promise. Evan loved the hue of persimmon and gold shimmering through the thick trees.

He drew in the primal scent of the lush evergreens surrounding them. The smell of moisture drawn in shades of gold and lilac slightly hinted the crisp winter snows were soon at hand. A gentle breeze wisping through the tall firs carelessly tossed Anne's hair freely about her face. From the moment he first saw Anne, Evan knew she would be his someday.

"I love walking," Anne shyly replied, barely glancing at

the teasing glint in Evan's dark eyes. Evan's lean, bronze, stature proudly portrayed the muscular fitness of the school's star basketball player. He knew he could have any girl he wanted. Yet something powerful attracted him to this shy, awkward girl who went out of her way to avoid his glances.

The intensity of his gaze made Anne's cheeks hot. The deep flush tinting her face made her troubled, dark satin eyes magnetic.

"Anne, I won't bite. Why don't you let me give you a lift home?"

Anne smiled politely, but her heart sank in panic. How could she let Evan Marcone give her a ride home? She was mortified to think he might find out where she lived. Why doesn't he just leave me alone, she thought moanfully.

Anne lived in a dingy alley adjoining an old, dirty, warehouse. She loved her brother, her sister, and she adored her mother. She didn't need anyone else, she defiantly thought, resolving to get rid of Evan.

Evan's father was the fire chief. Their beautiful home perched on a hill in an exclusive, lush area of town reflected his prominent position in the small community just outside of Pittsburgh. Anne knew his family would not tolerate her having any relationship with Evan. A girl from a broken home, living on the wrong side of the tracks, would be an embarrassment to Evan's family.

Her father, a working class, factory employee, deserted Anne and her family when she was only eight. Her mind drifted back to their last Christmas Eve together. She resentfully recalled the futility of her tears. She pleaded with her father not to leave them. Rocco's inability to put anyone else's well being before his own was not one of his outstanding virtues.

Although her feelings about him were primarily fear sprinkled with disgust, she was still afraid of what would happen to them if he left. She knew her mother's eye disease was progressively getting worse. It limited her vision and ability to work outside the home. An operation to correct her vision could not be performed for at least three years. Anne shuddered to think how they would survive.

Rocco's breath reeked of liquor, and his eyes never met hers. Funny, she couldn't remember his eyes ever meeting hers. Her only memories were of his drinking and his anger. Anne flashed with irritation as her mind recalled his belligerence in this state.

Her mother's routine when he came home obnoxious from a night out on the town was to make sure the kids were as quiet as possible. Then she'd prepare two scoops of ice cream placed directly in the middle of a whole cantaloupe cut in half. She'd fill each half of the melon generously with ice cream then quickly serve it to him. This usually settled him down enough to stop his intimidation.

Anne's stomach would churn as she trembled. She felt the cold claws of fear slide into her stomach while she tried to make herself as inconspicuous as possible to avoid his wrath. Her mother's gentle warning with her tender green eyes reminded Anne not to make any noise. If anyone should disturb his sleep, there would be hell to pay.

Marie, a feisty, outspoken Italian woman, attracted people with her open heart, her frank attitude, and engaging directness. She bellowed when she laughed, and always knew what to say when you needed someone to talk to. Her sincere, yet gutsy demeanor gave her four-foot, eleven-inch petite frame the appearance of a proud lioness. She still loved her husband regardless of his alcohol problem and the many other women in his life.

Rocco found his charisma with women his most valuable asset and didn't let his marriage cramp his style. Marie repeatedly swallowed her pride. She chose to look the other way and fiercely concentrate on her childrens' well-being.

Anne's mind jolted back to Evan. He firmly but politely gave it one last try. His pearl white teeth glistened as he flashed her his wide smile.

"Can I at least take you part way? This is the third time this week you've turned me down," he said as he jokingly pounded his chest. "Come on, give a guy a break," he teased.

Anne's eyes flickered, "Well, okay, but just take me to Main Street." She hesitated before opening the car door of his 1968 Mustang Convertible. Anne had never been in such a fabulous car before. The polish flawlessly gleamed a brilliant shade of red in the sunlight. Anne was impressed with the meticulous care Evan had taken with his pride and joy. She nervously drew in her breath and carefully opened the car door.

Evan possessed an unmistakable aura of command. He beamed with the pleasure of his conquest. He leaned back nonchalantly resting one arm on the door with his other hand confidently holding the top of the steering wheel. He arched his eyebrows and grinned. Anne's throat felt tight, and her trembling lips parched. She inhaled a mixture of warm fragrances of his cologne and the spice scented aroma of his car as she tried to relax.

"Anne, would you like to go to a movie tonight?" he boldly asked.

"Oh, no!" Anne quickly snapped. "I said you could take me to Main Street, nothing else." she sternly reminded him.

"Okay for now, Anne, but I'm not going to give up. I know you want to say yes. What's holding you back?" Evan's persistence surprised Anne.

Something in her stirred. "Evan, please be realistic. You and I live in two different worlds. It would never work," she stated frankly as the car pulled up to Main Street. "Thank you for the ride. I wish it could be different, but it just isn't."

She fumbled for her books and darted out of the car troubled by his determined attitude. He beeped and waved smiling as though she had accepted the date.

Anne shook her head walking with a light step, bewildered at the warm rush of bubbles running through her veins. The quick beat of her heart flooded her chest and tingled her limbs. A warm glow flowed to her face. A grin exploded on her lips then she sprang into a playful jog. She intermittently giggled and twirled the rest of the way home, delighted yet apprehensive about the handsome young basketball star.

That night, Marie noticed Anne's uneasy, strangely preoccupied mood. She gently prodded, "Is there something on your mind?"

Anne twisted her head from side to side trying to relieve the pressure from her stiff neck and tight shoulders. She looked squarely at her mother, "I'm going to get a job and get us out of this alley, Mom."

Marie's eyes looked at Anne cautiously. "Anne, you are just beginning high school. How will you be able to keep up with your studies and a job? Besides, who would hire a girl your age?"

"Don't worry about any of that, Mom. I know I can do it. I need to, Mom. I don't want to live in this alley the rest of my life. If I have an income, we can find a nicer place. I'm looking for a job tomorrow and somewhere to move."

Anne knew her mother was a proud woman. She worked long hard hours as a waitress in a local diner. For a short time after her operation, she washed dishes. When her eyesight became stronger, she moved up to a waitress position. Through her struggles to make ends meet, she focused on the rich blessings of loyal friends and the love of her family. However, her once radiant olive complexion now weathered the sallow look of fatigue and poverty.

Not wanting to offend her mother, she gently added, "I am proud of all your hard work, and I appreciate all you've done for me. I just think if I help out, our lives could be so much better. I love you, Mom."

Marie's eyes glistened realizing what a strong young woman her daughter was rapidly becoming. She hoped the hard life her children had to adjust to wouldn't dampen their spirit. She was glad to see Anne display the kind of spunk it took to survive but wished Anne could remain her little girl for just a while longer.

Marie didn't persist. She knew her daughter all too well. Once she put her mind to something, she wouldn't let it go. Marie looked lovingly at her daughter's determined face and quietly left Anne to her own thoughts.

Just as Anne had predicted, she pounded the pavement until she got a job. Rita, the manager of the local drive-in theater, felt compelled to give Anne a chance. Anne had been there every day letting Rita know how much she needed to work. Rita was impressed with her persistence.

Anne worked and saved her money then found a little blue guest house for rent on a nice street. The cottage was located behind the main house. It only had three small rooms. The kitchen, the largest room in the house, was warm and bright. Through the window you could see the long walkway that spiraled to the street. The walkway was surrounded by tall leafy emerald green trees that swayed as if dancing to the beat of the breeze. The kitchen was the most important room in the house for Anne's family. Marie especially liked to sit and drink her coffee in front of the kitchen window. Sitting around the kitchen table sharing their intimacies and their feelings with one another was an important part of each day.

Through the living room was an archway to the bedroom that would be shared by Anne, her sister, and her brother. It had barely enough room to squeeze in three twin beds and a dresser allowing skinny paths to move about. There was no bathtub, merely a sink and toilet. A thin partition extending only three quarters of the way up the wall was all that separated the bedroom from the bathroom.

The trap door on the floor in the bedroom opened into a cellar that had a shower. A cold, damp, moldy, smell permeated the dimly lit cellar. It was not a place one would want to linger for a long soothing shower.

The tiny house still held its charm for Anne, though. Her emotions wheeled with delight at the prospect of moving out of the alley. Anne's smile started at one side of her mouth then charged throughout her body. Anne was now ready for Evan. She finally would have a home she was not ashamed to show him.

The next two weeks were a whirlwind. Anne's cousins helped with the packing and moving. Marie was grateful she could always count on them in times like these. The transition was swift, smooth, and exciting. Dressed in her jeans and sweat shirt, Anne's tousled hair flew in her face as she lifted the end of the table with her brother. They laughed ignoring their exhaustion while tiny drops of perspiration dribbled down their faces. They were too happy about the move to let anything bother them.

The next week at school, Anne lingered at her locker hoping to see Evan. He usually made a point to see her each day after homeroom.

"Hi there, beautiful," Evan chirped.

Anne's white teeth flashed as she threw him a big smile. "Hi, Evan. I was hoping I'd see you today."

"Well, that is music to my ears." Evan's eyes were filled with Anne. He took in every feature of her smiling face. He chuckled and seized the opportunity to stand close to her in the crowded hall.

"Anne, how about going to the game Friday night?"

Anne's eyes smiled, "I'd love to, Evan."

Evan's face beamed. Anne finally accepted a date! He picked Anne up and twirled her around.

"Anne, you won't be sorry. We are going to have a good time together," he assured her. Then we'll go to dinner and a movie Saturday night," he pressed.

Anne giggled, "Why Evan Marcone, you sure don't waste any time when you put your mind to something, do you?" she teased. "That's one of the things I like most about you. I'm the same way. I have a feeling we are more alike than either of us realize. Friday and Saturday night sound great. I'm sure we'll have a good time no matter where we go," Anne added.

"You bet we will. You don't know how happy I am, Anne. I'll see you Friday night." Evan felt more exhilarated than he did at the last basketball game when his team creamed the opposing high school. He couldn't believe this girl made him feel happier than winning a game. He laughed out loud and shook his head.

"You're mine now, sweetheart," he whispered to himself smiling as he hurried to his next class.

Before they knew it, Anne and Evan began spending every spare moment together, laughing, talking, and confiding their hopes and dreams with one another. When Anne wasn't with Evan, she talked about him with her best friends, Donna and Dianna.

"Hey, Anne!" yelled Donna running over to her locker.

"Hi, Donna. I'm so glad it's Friday. We only have two more classes to go. Are you going to the game tonight?"

"You bet I am. I wouldn't miss this one. Are you going with Evan?"

Anne's eyes lit as she nodded. "I am so happy, Donna. I can't believe this is happening to me. Evan is so good to me. It's like we were meant to be together. We like the same things; we think the same thoughts. I feel so comfortable with him. I just wish his family liked me."

"Don't worry about it, Anne. They just don't know you. Once they do, they will fall in love with you."

Anne smiled, grateful to her friends who stood beside and encouraged her. But she felt that day would never come.

"Anne, I overheard Julie and Janie talking about you at lunch today. Be careful of those two. They are vicious, spoiled brats."

"Thanks for the advice, but I've already noticed that. Hey, I've got to run so I'm not late. Call me tonight before the game."

"Okay. See you later."

Evan also noticed the bad behavior of some of the snobby girls that lived near to him. He ignored their predictable snickers and snide comments. Although he protected Anne from their biting remarks as much as he could, they both still cringed at the callousness of their attitudes and their judgmental, personal attacks.

The couple even managed to weather the wrath of Evan's father for much longer than anyone thought possible. He refused to accept Anne or even acknowledge she was dating his son. Evan and Anne hoped that would change with time, but it didn't.

They decided to ignore it all. They went on long Sunday drives, teased and played with one another, went for quiet walks in the park, and spent cool evenings on the porch discussing all of life's possibilities.

The weeks, months, and next two years were swallowed in the swift current of time. Evan pulled Anne into his muscular arms, cradling her against his firm chest. The soft moonlight glided through the curtains. Anne's hands slid down his powerful back muscles carefully molding every inch of his tight, smooth flesh. Anne clung to him openly. She freely returned his unrestrained kisses, savoring the soft touch of his full lips, eager to feel his hands on her. Their young bodies touching, breathing, feeling each other was like a dam bursting with wild currents of energy. The discovery of their intriguing passions consumed them. "I love you, Anne," his soft, sensual lips whispered.

The rapid succession of her quick, deep breaths resembled a thunderstorm in the midst of raging rapids thrashing through a wild river. His fingers caressed her cheeks. He traced the delicate features of her face. Caressing her waist, he felt the last tremor race through her. The low sound of satisfaction from her soft, deep voice thrust forth the peak of his desire. The warmth of his body against hers made her tremble. His eyes lit with fire and passion as they grasped her eyes, piercing the depths of her soul. His coffee skin glistened with the sweet smell of perspiration trickling down his forehead.

They struggled to gain control. They both knew they needed to stop. He touched her arm and drew her back as his hand gently smoothed her ruffled hair. They both lay there silently, breathing in the aroma, memorizing, savoring every detail of that night. They deliberately printed a picture of each other in their minds to last forever knowing there were too many obstacles against them to overcome.

The war in Vietnam brought new pressures to the relationship. Evan's father, still adamantly opposed to their love, seized the opportunity as emotional blackmail. Evan's name was at the top of the list to be drafted unless he went to school. His father offered to pay for a good school in Pittsburgh as long as Anne was not a part of Evan's life. To make matters worse, Evan met and became attracted to a girl his family liked. He felt drawn to her and was worn down by the constant torment of his family's disapproval.

Anne and Evan began to argue over trite things. Each argument chipped away at the relationship. Anne sensed she was losing Evan, and there was little she could do to stop the process. "I love you too, Evan," she softly murmured.

"Anne, you'll never find anyone who will love you as much as I do. I just don't know how much longer we can last." Anne felt a strange, dark, sensation knowing he was probably right.

The cool breezes of autumn quickly turned into biting gusts of snow. The array of orange and red leaves swiftly trickled away leaving the barren arms of the trees stiff and cold. The usual animation and bright sparkle on Anne's face had withered away. Evan succumbed to family pressures and began school in Pittsburgh, and his new life with Lidia.

Anne's talks with her friends, Donna and Dianna, had abruptly changed from words of love and hope to sobs of misery and numbness.

Anne's eyes brimmed with tears as she swallowed hard. Life the past two months without Evan was unbearable. She lived in her fantasies of walking hand in hand in the park. Vivid memories of his sweet scent swept over her. The bitter reality that this was all in the past overwhelmed her. Her insides felt they were tossed on the ground and beaten with fists of anger. Her skin crawled at the thought of Evan caressing someone else.

I hate their narrow-minded, pompous attitudes. Who do they all think they are? Evan and I were good together. Her family and friends could see that. Why couldn't everyone else see the potential in her? Why did they have to be so cruel?

Someday, she vehemently vowed, *I'll be somebody.*

They'll all see! She felt her blood stirring. Her face tightened with anguish. She wanted to scream, to rip her bitter-sweet memories into shreads.

Her sobs crowded the room until it was difficult to breathe. Dragging herself up, she caught a glimpse of her swollen, tear-stained face in the mirror. It was bloated with pain and panic. A dizzying rush of anger seeped in her veins. She felt flushed and vulnerable to the world. I must get control of myself she resolved as she studied her reflection in the mirror. She prayed the volatile emotions swelling in her would subside.

She spent many hours in the church near her home. At first, she obsessedly prayed for Evan to come back. Eventually, she prayed for peace and the will to survive without him. She began taking long walks trying to shake off the foul mood that seemed to take over her personality.

She had to rely on the strength of her family until she regained her own. Each member of the family helped in their own unique ways. Her mother was a pillar of understanding and friendship. She used her sense of humor to get through the most difficult times in her life, and urged Anne to do the same.

"Anne, honey. I know how you hurt. You and Evan were such a good couple. Life isn't always fair or easy, but you have to make the best of things and move on. If you focus on the positive things in your life, with time, your pain will fade. I know that sounds impossible right now, but believe me. You are a strong girl, Anne. You'll get through this." Marie smiled at her daughter then shifted her attention to Nina tearing through the room running after Robert.

"Robert," Nina yelled, "give me back my shoe!"

Robert giggled. He dodged Nina by trying to hide behind Anne. He waved Nina's shoe in front of his face teasing her to come and get it.

Her brother, Robert, never ceased his teasing and pranks. His mischievous smile and impish laugh made Nina's fury dissolve into laughter. She reached over Anne to grab her shoe. Anne and Marie couldn't help but laugh too and were thankful Robert helped lift their spirits. They could always count on him for that. He ran around with the neighborhood kids who thought of Anne's house as a second home. Their sense of humor matched Robert's, so there was never a dull moment with them around.

Much to her surprise, Anne actually found herself laughing and joking around again. Although the pain did not cease, gradually her sleepless nights began to dissipate. She felt grateful for the help of her family and friends.

The gentle winds of the spring rain cleanly brushed the remaining face of winter away. The trees surrounding Anne's house began to stir with life. Their brilliant green foliage proudly swayed in rhythm with the heartbeat of the breeze.

The sunlight pouring through the trees made the porch glow in rich shades of red and blue. Thousands of yellow tones wisped through the thick leaves emitting powerful hints of golden, majestic glory.

The shimmering radiant light touched Anne's face as she sat on the swing alone. The breeze was clean and free lightly skipping across Anne's cheeks with the feathery softness of lace. Anne exhaled a deep audible breath expressing her restlessness.

She dodged the brutal thrust of loneliness by keeping herself busy at work and in school but could not evade its clenching grasp entirely. These past months without Evan felt lonely and empty, but she felt life within her starting to stir again. Filaments of golden red tones draped about her neck like seaweed as she released another sigh.

A leaf cracked yanking her attention to the sidewalk. A tall, lanky young man strode down the walkway tossing an undisturbed grin. Oh my God, Anne thought with panic, that's Jay Pantonne! She easily recognized his confident stride, his thick black hair and his thin, yet muscular frame.

Her body froze. Her eyes arched wide as their gazes interlocked with piercing magnetism. Little did Anne suspect this moment would be the beginning of her destiny. Jay approached the porch with a mischievous smile in his unflinching opaque black eyes. His prominently boned face proudly held his broad forehead and arrogant nose. His right cheek was slightly bruised from one of the many fights he had been in recently. His skin, slightly weathered to a manly texture, still held a glow of his deep rich tan.

I wonder what he's doing here, Anne thought. Maybe he has the wrong house, or maybe he's lost, she guessed feeling her body begin to fill with adrenaline. She frantically went through an exercise of pointless guesswork then tried to paint a calm look on her face. She tossed him a idle, quick glance with fear the rapid beat of her heart would reveal her panic.

Jay Pantonne's reputation as a lady's man with a hot fiery temper was well deserved. His violent, erratic behavior and the wild unsettled look in his eyes created an aura to be feared. It didn't take much to spur his quick temper into a violent rage. Yet, a mysterious sadness in his character and his confident, sensuous attitude made him strangely attractive.

"I just moved down the street, and I've noticed you walking. I thought I'd introduce myself. I'm Jay Pantonne."

As if you need an introduction, Anne thought not believing her ears. Why would Jay Pantonne want to introduce himself to her?

"And you are?" he prodded.

"I'm Anne," she replied slowly.

"Anne," he toyed with her name like a cat caging a mouse into a corner with juice flowing in its mouth, savoring every moment before his final prey. "Would you mind if I sat with you for awhile," he said not waiting for a reply.

Anne's mind whirled. "It looks like it doesn't matter if I mind or not," she replied sarcastically.

"You've got spunk. That's the kind of woman I like. I can tell we're going to get along just fine," he said with a glint in his eye.

"Speaking of getting along—why don't you? I'm just about to go in, and frankly, I'm not in the mood for company," she replied curtly.

"Tell me," he said, carefully eyeing every inch of Anne's body. "Why is a gorgeous lady like you out here alone to begin with? Where's your man?" he teased.

"That's none of your business, Mister Pantonne. Now if you'll excuse me." She abruptly stood up and turned to leave. She tossed a warning look over her shoulder, then he playfully caught her arm. She swallowed hard as his fingers contacted her bare arm. He laughed and sprang to the door first, mockingly opening it for her. He bowed with a large gallant gesture.

"There you go, madame. It looks like what you need is a good man to take that scowl off your face," he sneered as he pointedly strode in the opposite direction. She tried to laugh and make her voice sound strong.

"Well, if you know a good man, perhaps you can send him over," she taunted and quickly closed the door. She held her hand to her chest. She closed her eyes wondering how he had flared such emotions within her. Fighting to stabilize her heartbeat, she scowled at his impertinent nerve.

How dare he insinuate she needed a man! What an arrogant attitude, she angrily thought. She tried to dismiss the encounter, but his fiery eyes haunted her thoughts.

Later that evening, Marie approached Anne. "Anne, you seem restless. Is something bothering you?"

"No, nothing is bothering me, but you'll never guess who stopped by today."

"Did Evan come by?"

"No, Mom. I don't think Evan will ever stop by again," she said sadly. "Do you know a guy by the name of Jay Pantonne?"

Marie's face clouded, "What was he doing here? I've heard he's nothing but trouble, Anne. You be careful of him."

"Don't worry, Mom. I can take care of myself."

Nina walked in overhearing Jay Pantonne's name. "Anne, that guy is a womanizer, and I hear he has a terrible temper. I wouldn't get involved with him if I were you."

"Don't worry. We didn't hit it off anyway," Anne said thinking of Jay's dark sullen eyes wondering why they haunted her.

During the next month, Jay and Anne ran into each other on several occasions. At first, they bickered with each encounter.

As time passed, she yielded to his quick wit and began to soften. In spite of Nina and her mother's warnings, she felt drawn to him. She surprisingly found herself spending more time with Jay. They bantered incessantly in a battle of wits. Jay's sarcasm and Anne's defiant attitude consistently clashed. It seemed at times he made a point of ruffling her feathers.

In the quiet times, though, she slowly began confiding in him about Evan. Tears of envy still swelled in her eyes at the thought of Evan in someone's arms. Jay began showing the sensitive, softer side of himself he rarely let shine through. Before she realized, their peculiar acquaintance seemed to grow into friendship.

Spring gave way to the summer's moist, heavy, scorching hot days. The tall fan blowing hot air in Anne's living room was her only means of escape from the stagnant heat. Suffocating humidity burned into the nights with exhausting persistence. Anne wiped the sweat from her brow and lifted her hair from the back of her head to fan her dripping neck.

The end of the month is my seventeenth birthday, she thought. A restless gnawing often intruded her thoughts these days. She graduated from high school and worked as a secretary in a small office in the day, keeping her job at the drive-in a few nights a week. She appreciated the income, but the work did not satisfy her. She couldn't put her finger on it but felt something was missing in her life. An unsettling fire festered inside her igniting her passion for excitement and adventure.

"Anne, the phone's for you," her brother called.

"Thanks, Rob." Anne heard Jay's voice when she picked up the phone.

"Hi, Anne. Listen—there's a good movie on TV tonight. My parents are out of town, and I have this big house to myself. I sure could use some company. How about coming over?"

Anne hesitated.

"Come on," he urged her, "I'll make some popcorn."

"Okay, I'll come by in about an hour," she replied.

"I'll see you then, Anne."

Jay hung up the phone then leaped up the stairs to his room. His mother worked for the school and his father at the factory. Their home was old but large and well kept. His light blue room with navy accents easily held the four poster bed between his desk and night stand. He walked to the window and pulled the shades closed. A pale yellow glow seeped in from the street light below. He stopped and smiled at his reflection in the large mirror attached to his dresser.

"Anne, you're going to become a real woman tonight." He had waited long enough and knew she was hot. He could feel the fire in her eyes. Besides, her body was too good to waste. "You don't know what to do with that body or your passion yet, Anne, but I'm going to show you tonight," he said with a grin. He straightened his shirt collar and excitedly ran down to answer the door.

Jay smiled confidently. He poured on his Italian charm throughout the evening. He looked at her supple body, her delicate fingers, and smelled her sensuous perfume. He looked into her large brown eyes and decided it was time to put his plan into action.

He caught Anne's hand as she reached for the popcorn. His fingertips brushed over her palm, and his mouth swooped to surround her lips. She instinctively drew back, arching her eyebrows in surprise. Stunned with the force of Jay's movement, she put her finger to her bruised lip and shook her head. This was not the gentle loving caress she had experienced with Evan or one of Jay's usual playful kisses.

His heavy arms urgently clamped tightly around her. He grunted and positioned Anne on to the floor with the swift precision of a man who had done this a thousand times before. Anne writhed and twisted to free, her mouth clenched by his grip. She gagged, gasped for air, and tried to heave his heavy body away. His crushing weight held her down while he kissed her straining flesh. Her legs were imprisoned by the pressure of his hips and legs. He grunted, wedging her jaw wide with increasing pressure, oblivious to her objections.

"Anne," he panted with hot, quick breaths, "I know you

want me—don't fight it. Just relax." Sweat dripped from his brow. His grin hardened. Feeling a cold, tight clench of disbelief seep through her bones, she became paralyzed with scorching confusion.

Surely her repugnance was evident on her face. What had she done to provoke this? Was her top revealing too much? Was her skirt too short? Did she tease him too much with her kisses and flirting? What could she say to make him stop? I'll lay perfectly still, she thought with desperation.

"Don't worry, baby, this won't hurt. I'd never do anything to hurt you, Anne." She closed her eyes and sniffed back her tears knowing her plan was futile. She painfully recalled the last time she had heard these words. She was only twelve.

A shiver ran into her veins. Images surfaced of the putrid warehouse worker who violated her. He claimed he needed a glass of water one day when she was alone. She thought it was peculiar, but let it pass. He locked the door behind him and said those same words to her before he ripped off her blouse and placed his mouth on her breasts.

"I'm just showing you what your husband will do when you grow up," he grunted. She vividly recalled the sour scent of onion on his breath. "You don't have a father to show you these things," he hissed as she cried and begged him to stop.

Anne felt dirty and embarrassed when she told her mother later. To avoid further embarrassment, her mother bargained with Pete—silence for his promise never to come near them again. Marie was convinced there was no punishment suitable for this crime. Having to bargain with him sickened her.

"I'll kill you, you bastard, if you ever come near one of my kids again. Do you understand me?" Marie's voice snarled. Her nostrils flared while she angrily spit the vicious words boiling from her lips. She hoped her threat would scare the slime away. The violation of her daughter burned so deep, she did intend to keep her threat if he ever came near one of them again.

Anne's mind jolted back. Jay swiftly entered her before she could think of a way to stop him. She lay there still and quiet, dimly feeling the pain and humiliating destruction of her pride. She knew if anyone found out what had happened, they'd think she got exactly what she deserved. After all, didn't everyone warn her about him? They'd all think she was no better than a slut. Jay lifted his head. He waited in disbelief, puzzled at the cold icy stare he received after he gave Anne the privilege of being a real woman for the first time.

A rancid odor filled Anne's head with nausea. Eyes cast to the floor, she blindly covered herself and listlessly walked toward the door. With her hand on the doorknob, she yanked her head around.

"Is this what I've been waiting for all my life? I've always heard how great sex is. Either that's a lie or you're a lousy lover. What a disappointment," she slurred with a curled lip and a vengeful smile wanting to hurt him as much as possible. She walked out and tossed her head defiantly, not bothering to close the door.

Five months later, Anne stood at the stairs of the airplane, her lips quivering in a smile. Marie's face was drawn with anguish watching her daughter try to mask her fear.

God bless you, my little Anne, she silently despaired. She looked at her daughter's slightly swollen stomach wanting to claw the hair from Jay's scalp. Never had she hated so deeply before. She had to send her baby away because of that dirty son-of-a-bitch, she vengefully thought.

After Anne's father, now living in Sacramento, refused to help, Marie made arrangements for Anne to temporarily stay with a cousin in San Francisco. Marie's heart sank as she watched her daughter leave. She felt trapped and helpless like a caged animal in a testing lab before a gruesome experiment.

She couldn't let anyone know Anne's condition. Her life would be ruined in this small town. No man would touch her or marry her if they found out that scum had his way with her. She had to go away and hide this hideous situation. They couldn't afford a baby anyway, she rationalized fearing the baby could turn out to be crazy like his father. NO, she resolved. There is no alternative. Since Anne refused an abortion, she must give this child away.

Marie leaned on her daughter, Nina, for strength. Her knees felt like fluid, and her stomach churned. She knew her nights would be filled with sleepless panic, pain, and anguish until Anne was home safe again.

Her eyes met Anne's before she turned around to board the plane. Marie blew her a kiss and read Anne's lips. "Good-bye, Mom," she whispered. A tremor flushed through Anne's body, and a feeling of dread rushed in her veins. She groped for strength suddenly feeling her backbone melt. She desperately repressed the urgent need to cry. She vowed with fierce determination to rise above the turn of events in her life. However, she was afraid to guess what this journey into madness would bring. Somehow she knew she would never be home again.

Chapter Two

SAN FRANCISCO—1970-1974

The reception in San Francisco was hardly what Anne expected. Anne's cousin, Cecelia, failed to mention her husband, Bruce's, hostile opposition to Anne moving in. She found herself in the middle of a war zone. Within a month, Cecelia conceded to Bruce's demands and asked Anne to leave.

"Anne, I know I told your mother you could stay here, but my husband is making it too uncomfortable. I'm sorry, but you need to find some place else to stay, and you need to do it this week."

"Cecelia, I don't know anyone here except Tracey! She has invited me to parties at her apartment when she sees me walking in the day, but we aren't friends." Anne felt stunned.

Losing all sense of security so close to her delivery terrified her. "I've stopped in a few times, but I hardly know her."

"Yes, I know who she is. Anne. You've visited her enough to know her. I think it's perfect. I heard she was looking for a roommate. Why don't you go by this evening and see if she still needs one?" Cecelia said hurriedly leaving the room to avoid Anne's eyes and any further conversation.

That night the arrangements were made. Considering the limited choices at this time, and Cecelia's rush to get rid of her, Anne packed her bags. Too proud to let on how terrified she really was, she pasted a calm look on her face and quietly left to spend the last two months of her pregnancy with Tracey.

With suitcase in hand, Anne walked down to Tracey's apartment. The shimmering sun glowed through the clear sea blue sky unlike the heavy smoke-filled sky tinged with gray-black tones in the Pittsburgh area. The polluting steel mills replaced clean oxygen in the area with tainted brown air and a steamy overcast of black glaze.

Anne breathed in the calm breeze of March. It brushed her face with warm softness of a fresh season, but she still felt alone and frightened. Anne noted how the lush beauty of dense tall rows of palm trees contrasted the run-down condition of the apartment building. Walking always lifted her spirits but not this time. She felt heavy and more alone than ever. She put down her suitcase. She hesitated before knocking then tapped lightly on the door.

Tracey slowly answered the door after Anne's third knock. "Come on in," she said nonchalantly waddling her plump body to the nearest seat.

Anne entered the sparsely furnished living room. The coffee table, stained with rings of red wine, was cluttered with odds and ends. An afghan covered the green plaid couch trying to hide dirt and holes beneath. The air smelled dusty and stale.

"I've lived alone a long time, Anne, and I prefer it that way," Tracey curtly commented. She looked at Anne's stomach and her one suitcase openly turning down the corners of her lips.

"I want you to understand the only reason I'm taking you in is because I'm low on cash at the moment. The small bedroom is yours. We have to share the bathroom. Make sure you clean up your own mess and buy your own food. Pay your rent the first of each month, and we'll get along just fine. Please don't think of this as a long term relationship, Anne. I hope to be back on my feet in six months. Then you're on your own."

The next two months dragged by. Tracey and Anne's relationship became increasingly strained with each passing day. Anne spent most of her time in her room or walking around the apartment complex. She tried to avoid Tracey whenever it was possible.

The pressure of the baby against her ribs and the baby's movements uncomfortably increased daily. Her back ached incessantly, and her legs burned from her newly acquired protruding varicose veins. The tight bulge in her stomach dropped slightly each day making her insides feel like she was about to explode. Dark circles under her eyes from lack of sleep stole the color from her face.

She usually avoided touching her rounded stomach but hesitantly ran her hand lightly over it. A chill ran through her. She realized the only feeling she had was a numb, empty ache. She had no warm feelings for this child or for herself.

She dearly missed her friends and family, but she held no hope of ever going home or of life ever being the same. She quickly brushed away the tear trickling down her cheek. A feeling of loneliness pierced through the numbness. She counted the days until this terrible ordeal was over.

Anne, not accustomed to the nightly late-into-the-morning parties, booze, and drugs of her roommate became run down and depressed. Already agitated with Anne's distaste of her behavior and the increased tension in their relationship, Tracey screeched when Anne called for help in the middle of one of Tracey's many parties. Since Anne did not know what to expect or have anyone to explain the stages of labor and delivery to her, she panicked when her water broke. Instead of helping, Tracey's chubby face exploded in red blotches to match her brightly lit eyes, pulsating with fury.

"Anne, I'm not your nursemaid. Call your doctor and call a cab," she huffed. Then pack all of your things, you stupid bitch, and get out, and give me your key," she hissed. "I don't want you and your pompous attitude back here. You've got a lot of nerve putting your nose up to me. Your attitude has irritated me from the minute you started whining about my lifestyle. I'm not the one pregnant and unmarried," she slurred with a haughty, dismissing glance.

"Don't look so pathetic. You're just having a baby. You're not the first woman to have one, you know. I'm just glad I don't have to put up with you anymore."

Anne, nauseated by the red blotches burning into Tracey's plump face, mustered up just enough energy to call Tracey a bitch. Her attention then focused on a sharp pain in her back and stomach. She quickly gathered her things and called a cab.

Anne's dark eyes traveled quickly across the room. She stood uncomfortably in the midst of the rushed hospital attendants and nauseating odors. After she managed to fill in the necessary paper work, she found a chair. Her face riveted in pain and frustration while she slumped in a chair waiting for help. The hospital was soaked with hurried frenzy. Anne grew irritated with the lack of attention she received. She was about to complain when a nurse scurried over to her.

"You'll have to take this cot in the hall. We're all filled up," the nurse quickly stated with a cynical frown and hardly apologetic tone.

She stood staring at the cot in disbelief. Rampant thoughts pounded in her head. What am I going to do? I have nowhere to go. How can this be happening to me? Her eyes, stinging with tears, reflected fear and panic.

The next four hours crept in agonizing slow motion while her pain sharply increased. Her insides throbbed and her head wheeled. She heard a disgusting groan slither from the back of her throat forcefully increasing in volume before it escaped her lips. Suddenly, Anne's head jerked with the pressure to push as the nurse's hand twisted inside her. Consumed with pain, she choked. She heard the nurse's voice yell frantically. "Don't push—do you hear me—don't push. Your doctor's one hour away. The umbilical cord is wrapped around your baby's neck. If he comes out now, he might choke to death!"

Anne reacted impulsively to the next pain. She begged for help while the hovering nurse held the baby inside. "Please, God, help me!" Anne pleaded. Darkness engulfed her whirling head.

Faintly she heard a voice ringing, "We're losing her doctor!" Anne, too exhausted to fight the darkness, let it wisp her away like a giant eagle into oblivion.

She slipped in and out of consciousness during the next three days from her hard labor and excessive blood loss. The woman in the next bed looked sympathetically at her tiny frame lying lifeless and her once creamy complexion now gaunt and pasty. She sadly wondered if anyone cared about this young girl and what would happen to her.

SACRAMENTO 1970

Meanwhile in Sacramento, Marsha and Jake freshly painted the baby's room in pale green. A yellow border of bears and ducks matched the curtains and blanket Marsha made. The wooden crib and dressing table were neatly made up and ready for their new arrival.

All the paperwork for the adoption was in order. Her baby was inside a young woman just about ready to deliver. They were told little about the birth mother and father except they were of Italian descent. Jake and Marsha were tickled with that information because of Jake's time spent in Italy on business trips. He fell in love with their country and culture. He hoped to bring his family to visit Italy one day. Marsha secretly hoped for a boy, but would be happy either way. They liked the names Denise or Richard but decided to wait until they saw the baby to pick a middle name.

Marsha's thoughts drifted to the fresh flowers she placed on Tony and Joey's, graves yesterday. After two miscarriages due to the Rh factor, Jake and Marsha decided to adopt. Marsha pictured her two son's frail, tiny bodies. She visualized how their two perfect little faces would be smiling up at her if they had lived. She held them in a special place in her heart.

Their seven year old, Jessica, was as excited as Marsha about the new baby coming. "Mommy, will the baby love me?" Jessica asked with wide solemn eyes.

"Oh course, honey. Who wouldn't love my little sweetheart?" Marsha chuckled. Marsha was pleased as she put the finishing touches in the room.

Marsha's short brown hair matched her glowing eyes. Her blue sweater proudly showed off her rounded figure. She held her five-foot, three-inch frame with self-assured determination. She could barely contain her excitement and anticipation to hold her beautiful baby in her arms.

"God, I already love you," she tenderly thought smiling. Jake softly kissed her forehead. He watched her face beam with a soft warm glow of a mother-to-be. She elevated one brow, lifting her chin for a kiss and playfully giggled as their lips met. "I love you, Jake," she purred.

Jake smiled, "I love you too, honey." Their heads turned when Jessica came skipping into the room humming. Jake swooped up Jessica and held her in the air. They played and laughed until they were exhausted then tucked Jessica in for the night.

Marsha tenderly massaged Jake's back and ran her fingers through his thick hair. He propped himself up on his elbow. A smile faintly crossed his lips. Gently, he outlined her face with his fingers then kissed her eager lips. Her eyes glowed with invitation. He folded her into his arms savoring the warmth of their bodies molding together. Their passion flowed through them during the night until they fell asleep in the softness of each other's arms.

The next morning the long awaited call came. "Hello, Mrs. Tess, congratulations. He's an eight-pound, five-ounce beautiful baby boy." Marsha's heart leaped. Hysterical laughter bubbled to her smiling lips.

"Mrs. Tess," the voice lowered, "there was a complication at birth. The baby's umbilical cord prolapsed. It wrapped around his neck restricting oxygen to his brain. There is a chance the baby will be developmentally delayed and have other complications. The severity of damage to the brain cannot be fully determined until the child is at least two years or older." A shudder overwhelmed Marsha's body while a cold fist of fear enclosed her heart. Tears welled in the back of her eyes losing their battle to a hot flash of fury.

"What exactly does this mean?" she questioned locating her composure. "I've waited a long time for your agency to match me with the right child, and I've waited through the last three months of this mother's pregnancy. He's already my baby in my heart. I know I haven't even seen him yet, but I still feel a bond with this child. I don't care what's wrong with him. He's my baby," her voice strongly emphasized. "I just need you to explain all the details to me, so I know how to care for him and what to expect." How could this happen to her long awaited son? she agonized. Please, Lord, make him strong and well. I can't survive another tragedy, she panicked.

"I'll read you part of the medical report I received. 'Cerebral hypoxia was caused by the umbilical cord prolapsing and wrapping around the baby's neck limiting the amount of oxygen reaching the baby's brain. Damage may be localized to particular areas of the brain causing specific defects of brain function ranging from problems of minor loss of coordination or speech difficulty to mental and physical handicaps such as cerebral palsy. The infant is in guarded condition, but generally does not exhibit any chronic conditions. No disability is noted at this time, and a complete diagnosis cannot be rendered at this early stage'...I'll meet with you this afternoon, and we'll go over everything."

Stunned, Marsha slowly walked away from the phone. "We'll get through this, Richard, just hang in there baby," she softly breathed. She dropped to her knees and silently prayed.

SAN FRANCISCO HOSPITAL—1970

Back in the San Francisco hospital, Anne groggily began to stir.

"Hello there," a strange yet friendly voice said. Anne tilted her head toward the voice trying to focus her heavy eyes. Every limb felt as though she had been run over by a truck. Her muscles cried and pulled her back as she attempted to sit up. With palms sweating and stomach grinding, she stifled a moan.

"I was wondering if you'd ever wake up. Do you know where you are, honey?"

Anne, still trying to focus, slowly nodded.

"I know your name is Anne. I'm Millie. You delivered your baby a few days ago. You sure have been through a rough one. I'm glad to see you're coming out of it," she said with a smile. "Your baby is still in guarded condition but getting stronger every day," she added hesitantly.

Anne's shoulders slumped dejectedly. I'm not in the mood for a conversation, she thought, sliding toward anger and self-pity. She sniffed back her tears. "It's nice to meet you Millie. Forgive me if I'm not much company," she said in a listless voice, ignoring the comment about the baby.

"Look sweetie, I understand. The nurses filled me in on your situation. I'm sorry anyone has to be put through something like that. I was wondering, do you have a place to go after you're discharged?"

Anne bit her lip glancing bitterly out the window. Shades of gray predominated the overcast clouds hovering in the distance. The heavy sky mimicked the cold darkness and hollow feeling in her heart.

"No, I don't," her voice trailed off wistfully. Swallowing hard, she fought off the panic surging through her breast.

"Well, I know of a one room flat that's inexpensive. It's not in the best area of town, but it might suit you until you get on your feet. Think about it, and let me know if you're interested," she kindly offered.

"There's nothing to think about," Anne said decisively.

"At least it would be a roof over my head, and it has to be better than the last two places I've been." Her voice softened, "Thank you, Millie. You're an angel," she replied, touched by this stranger's kindness.

During the next three weeks Anne had to stay in bed taking iron shots weekly to recover. She needed her mother to help her since she was unable to get out of bed much. As soon as Anne called, Marie borrowed money to fly in to help her. When she was able, Anne learned the bus system and began looking for a job.

The three weeks Marie spent with her flew by. Marie and Anne had long talks about everything but carefully avoided the subject of Anne's baby. Marie filled Anne in on all that was going on back home and reminisced. She tried to convince Anne to come home with her but realized it was useless. Marie was relieved Anne at least found a job, as a secretary with an insurance company, before she had to leave.

"Anne, since you're feeling stronger, why don't we do something fun before I leave."

"Yes, I'm definitely in the mood for some fun, and I'm feeling much stronger."

She thought for a minute then smiled. "I have an idea. Why don't we go to Hollywood to see if we run into any famous people. We can get a motel for the night, then we can go to Disneyland the next day. Neither one of us has ever been there. Don't you think it would be fun?"

"I love it, Anne. Are you sure you're up to that much excitement?"

"Mom, I'm going to go crazy if I don't get out and do something fun. Let's go for it."

"All right. You're on. We'll find out the bus schedule and go tomorrow. We'd better get to bed early, though. It's going to be an exhausting weekend."

Anne loved to look at Marie's large green eyes when she became excited. They glowed with the delight of a child and the sparkle of a rainbow.

"Okay. Let's call the bus terminal then hit the sack. I can hardly wait until tomorrow," Anne sang.

Morning rushed in. Anne and Marie had a light breakfast then headed for the bus. The ride was long but didn't bother either one of them. They were so busy talking and laughing they couldn't believe how quickly the time went by.

"I'm so excited, I can't see straight," Anne chirped. "What are we going to do if we see a movie star?"

"I'll go right up to him and ask for an autograph," Marie boldly stated giggling.

"Okay. I'll be right behind you."

By the time the bus pulled into Hollywood, Marie and Anne were famished.

"The first thing we have to do is eat," Marie said.

"Mom, can you believe we are on Hollywood Boulevard! We have to go to Sunset Strip. I hear Lana Turner was discovered in a little diner there."

Anne's senses tingled. Overwhelmed with the excitement in the air, Anne stopped in front of the theater to look at the stars' handprints in the sidewalk. The street seethed with a variety of strange people wondering about. They were stopped three times within a matter of moments by people with white gauze wrapped around their heads in a cone shape begging for money.

"Mom, look at the people carrying picket signs and yelling in front of the theater." Their wide eyes gawked in curiosity, but they decided not to get too close to the angry crowd.

"I don't believe it," Marie said in astonishment. "This place is something else. I hope there's a restaurant nearby. I'm starved."

"How's this restaurant look, Mom?" Anne said a few minutes later.

"It looks clean. I think it will be fine."

They were so hungry, everything on the menu looked great. Marie always had her cup of coffee first, so Anne ordered a soda while waiting for the meal.

"Look, Anne, that's Chad Everett from the doctor series on TV," Marie excitedly said as she got up to approach him.

Anne smiled watching her mother shake the popular, handsome, TV actor's hand with confident, friendly ease. She heard her mother's frisky, deep laugh and grinned widely. Marie turned to Anne and motioned waving her arm for Anne to come over.

Anne's beat red face exploded in perspiration. She found herself walking toward the gorgeous actor and her mother. Marie introduced them as though she had known him all her life. He smiled graciously and gave her an autograph. It was evident he was quite charmed with Marie.

Scurrying back to the table Anne laughed, "Mom, you're crazy. I would never have had the nerve to go over without you. That was great. You'll have to tell everyone back home. They'll never believe it." Anne and Marie huddled in their booth giggling with excitement.

Marie chuckled, "You have more guts than you know, Anne. Someday you'll realize just how strong you are. You know, Anne, I have an old friend from Pittsburgh's address and phone number with me. You used to play with his daughter, Marilee, when you were younger. They moved to California about ten years ago. I'd like to leave the number with you in case you ever want to call them."

"That sounds good, Mom. I do remember Marilee quite well. It's nice to know someone is nearby that is from our part of the universe." She took the information and placed it in her wallet.

After finishing her meal, Anne took the napkin from her lap and dabbed her lips. She then spied a waitress carrying a mouth watering, huge strawberry shortcake with gobs of ice cream and whipping on the top.

"Oh, that looks too good to pass up. Do you think we can handle one? Look at those strawberries. I've never seen strawberries that big."

Marie looked at the desert and agreed with Anne. It did look too good to pass up. They decided to split one.

"I'm about ready to explode," Anne said taking the last bite of the rich vanilla ice cream.

Marie smiled. She leaned back to loosen her belt, "Me too, but it was great. Why don't we walk around for awhile to work off some of this and maybe do some shopping?"

"All right. You never have to break my arm to go shopping. I'm ready."

The clothes in each shop were different but equally as beautiful. Marie and Anne scanned the entire Hollywood Boulevard area and hit Beverly Hills. By the end of the day, they flopped into bed. They fell asleep while talking about the day.

It seemed as though Anne barely closed her eyes when the sun piercing through the thin curtain of the cheap hotel room woke her. Anne normally liked to sleep late in the mornings but was glad to get an early start. They both tingled with excitement about their Disneyland trip.

They enjoyed every part of Disneyland. Anne's favorite part of their Disneyland adventure, "It's a Small World," brought a wide grin to her face. She felt carefree and happy singing along to the tune with the small voices. Marie harmonized with Anne feeling like a child again. They roared with laughter in the Pirates of the Caribbean ride when water splashed their faces and were amazed at the life-like qualities of each character.

They ran from one ride to another like school children, took every photo opportunity, ate something from each stand that tempted them, and shopped.

Anne noticed some great big white floppy hats. After trying several on, she picked out the biggest one her head could hold. "With this wild hat, and my new sunglasses, I look just like everyone else here in California." she said modeling her new look.

Marie and Anne both giggled. They made sure to get a picture with a Disney character and Anne's big hat to show people at home.

"Anne, do you feel strong enough to stay one more night so we can see Knott's Berry Farm tomorrow? I read in the paper that Ricky Nelson and the Righteous Brothers are performing there."

"You're kidding. We are definitely going to stay for that. Your plane doesn't leave for two days, so we have the time."

"I wish Nina and Robert could see all of this. Please give them a big hug for me, and tell them I love them and miss them when you go home, okay?"

"Of course I will, honey. You know they miss you too," Marie said misty-eyed.

On the bus ride back to San Francisco, Anne and Marie raved about the great performances of Ricky Nelson and the Righteous Brothers. They talked about all the strange and wonderful things they saw and did.

"I'll never forget this time we had together, Mom. You know I can't come home. There's just too many bad memories I can't deal with. But someday I'll have my own place. I'd like to get you and Nina and Robert out of that town, so we can all have a better life together. Someday, we'll all be together again. I promise you that."

The determined resolution and strong look on Anne's face made Marie believe in the possibility of it happening someday. She hugged her daughter. "You never know what God has in store for you, Anne. I think anything is possible. In the meantime, you make sure to remember we all love you very much, and you can come home any time."

"I know, Mom. I guess we better pack your things for tomorrow. I hate to see you leave. I don't want you to worry about me, though. I'm going to be just fine."

The next morning Anne hugged her mother at the airport.

"Take care of yourself, honey. Be careful out here. You know I'm not too good at writing letters but write to me often," her mother tenderly insisted.

She nodded solemnly and clung to her mother's tight embrace. Marie smiled, but her face reflected fear and concern.

"Good-bye, Mom. I love you," Anne called before her mother boarded the plane. She shot a stinging glance toward the plane as it took off. Her eyes, brilliant with apprehension, narrowed. She moved slowly away. Conflicting emotions of loneliness, anxiety, and cold anger ran through her bones.

She wished she could go home. But things were different now. She was different. How she wished she could be with Evan and spend the rest of her life with him in the security and warmth of his love.

It's too late for that now, she thought in dismay. He's moved on with his life, and that's what I have to do. Driven by the instinctive need for survival, she took hold of herself and plodded back to the flat.

Over the next six months, Anne's attitude changed drastically. Her dreams faded into disillusionment. She turned to drugs and sex to dull her senses and soothe her weary heart.

"Take another hit, Anne," Barry said, deeply inhaling then holding his breath. Anne did look up her old friend, Marilee. They quickly rekindled their childhood relationship, and Marilee introduced Anne to some of her friends, and to drugs. The thought of drugs disgusted her when she lived with Tracey, but the relief they offered her from reality now was a welcomed escaped. Anne cared deeply for Marilee and Barry. She felt she could not have survived the past months without their support, but still missed home. She felt restless and unfulfilled.

"Just one more is about all I can handle," Anne slurred with glazed dilated eyes.

Coughing from the burning sensation in his lungs, Barry's face broke into a wide, comical grin. Hysterical laughter barreled from Anne until her face and sides ached. By the time she stopped laughing, she forgot what was so funny to begin with.

"This is great..." Anne started to say attempting to get off the floor to move to the couch. Uncrossing her legs, shakily swaying as she attempted to stand, she groped to steady herself on the couch's arm with one hand.

"Barry, the room is whirling..." her voice trailed. The next thing she knew, she opened her eyes and was alone in the dimly lit, cluttered room. Noting pieces of her clothing strewn about, she reached for a robe. Wondering if it was still night or morning, she slowly got up to look at the clock. Her hand automatically went to her head to quiet her throbbing temples as she stood. She headed straight for water to get rid of the feeling of cotton in her mouth. She crinkled her nose in dismay at the clock above the sink. It reminded her it was time to get ready for work.

I feel like shit, she thought with irritation. "I don't know how I'm going to make it through today," she mumbled, dragging herself into the shower.

Warm water pulsated on her head and neck relieving some tension and aggravation. She deeply inhaled the heavy steam attempting to soothe her irritated lungs. Bitterly frustrated with the shape her life had taken, she deliberately relaxed each muscle in her neck one by one. She focused on the hot stream of pulsating water. Reluctantly she forced herself out of the shower to dress for work and heard the phone ring. She wrapped a towel around her body and one around her hair then sprinted toward the phone.

"Hello, Anne," she heard a friendly tone. "This is your Uncle Abe from Austin. I just talked to your mother and decided to give you a call. She's feeling uncomfortable with you in that big city all by yourself. Would you consider coming to Austin for awhile to see how you like it? You can stay with us for awhile. If you decide to stay, there are many nice apartments nearby. The weather here is fabulous, and it's a great little city."

"Uncle Abe, that is so nice of you. I'd love to come for awhile. I would have to clear it with my work. I need a job to come back to if I don't like it there. But I'd love to give it a try. I'll give you a call once I've made arrangements." Anne hung up with a contented sigh. Although he moved away when Anne was young, she remembered his quick wit and sense of humor. She liked the sound of his friendly voice and warm invitation.

Maybe this is just the break I need to make a new beginning for myself. I can't go on the way I am, she thought.

Maybe moving from here will take my mind off the baby. I signed the adoption papers, so there is no turning back. All he'll ever have of me is the St. Christopher medal I gave him. I wonder if he'll ever look at it and think of me? I wonder if he'll be normal after losing so much oxygen to his brain. I'm glad I didn't look at him after he was born. Without a face to haunt me, maybe I can forget. She shook her head resolving to quickly put everything in order to begin her new life in Austin.

Having little to pack, Anne left San Francisco as abruptly as she came without a backward glance. She had a good feeling about Austin, and by now she had learned to trust her instincts. Austin was love at first sight.

"My God, look at those stars! I've never seen anything like it," Anne breathed gazing at the sky. It glittered with brilliant lights resembling tiny twinkling apples of silver in a setting of gold.

Anne's aunt and uncle laughed and were happy she liked Austin. They knew Marie would sleep better knowing Anne was in a safer environment.

Anne thought contentedly. I'm going to love it here. I have finally found some place that feels like it could be home. She admired Uncle Abe's courage to move to Austin, his thirst for knowledge and his determination to get a college education. She hoped she could someday be as successful as he was.

She was also excited because her cousins from Pennsylvania recently moved nearby. It would be great if the rest of my family could move here too, she thought with hopeful anticipation. Then Austin would really feel like home.

Anne quickly settled in. Within a few months she found a job, a small apartment, and some friends. Anne created a new look for herself. Much to her aunt and uncle's chagrin, she shortened her skirt length to bring attention to her shapely legs and reshaped her eyebrows giving her lively dark eyes a more refined look. Her disposition reflected the good feeling she had about Austin. She walked with a hint of adventure and self-assurance. Her creamy features, bronzed by the Austin sun, glistened with rich tones. A golden blaze in her dark eyes ignited with mischief and excitement.

The magnetism she drew, and the attentiveness and open admiration men displayed pleased her. She had been deserted, jilted, defiled, and humiliated by the crushing blows of the men in her past. She intended to make sure that was not going to happen again. The only way she knew how to relate to a man was through her sensuality. Being wickedly fascinating was a far tastier morsel than the hell she had been through.

Never again would she allow herself to be put in a position to beg for love or experience the pain and degradation of desertion. She vowed to carefully guard her façade, to protect the sensitive, naive girl from a little town back East still breathing underneath her self-assured mask. She deliberately determined not to allow that part of her to be taken advantage of again.

Anne didn't count on the possibility of falling in love. She believed Evan would be the only man she would ever love. She still longed for his strong arms to sweep her away. She cherished the memory of his scent, his smile, his light touch. His darkly handsome features burned in her mind. She closed her eyes. She brought her fingers to her lips tracing them lightly like Evan did so many times. She could almost feel his finger against her pulsating lips.

"A penny for your thoughts," Marco whispered in Anne's ear standing behind her.

Jolted by his untimely intrusion of her thoughts, Anne jumped.

"I didn't mean to startle you," he chuckled, playfully squeezing her arm.

Anne turned around to face Marco. Her irritation disappeared when she saw his impish grin.

"Anne," Marco said as he straightened the bow under her work collar. "I have tickets for a concert tonight. Please go with me."

The light in Marco's eyes and the flash of his wide grin melted Anne's heart. This was Marco's third attempt to get

Anne on a date. She felt he would not give up until she said yes. Anne liked self-confidence in a man and a willingness to pursue what he wanted. His audacious persistence reminded her of Evan and impressed her.

"All right. That sounds great." Looking into his beaming face and sparkling eyes, Anne was glad she accepted the date. There was something special and different about Marco. He was bright, charming, and intensely determined to make Anne a part of his life. He was more serious than the other men Anne was seeing. He studied long hours to get accepted into law school. He displayed the kind of fierce determination needed to succeed. Although she respected the intense, anxious, serious side of Marco, she fell in love with his quick wit and brilliant sense of humor.

Marco swept Anne in a whirlwind of attention, making no attempt to disguise his admiration. He inundated her with flowers, candy, exciting dates, and romance. He looked at her in a way no other man, except Evan, had before. His green eyes glowed with insatiable desire for Anne. Before she realized, she had no time or energy to spend on anyone else. As much as she didn't want to be vulnerable to another person, she couldn't resist Marco's relentless insistence and persistent pursuit.

"Anne, I want us to be together forever. I want our futures to be together. I am going to make it big in this world, Anne, and I want you to be by my side."

The urgency in his voice and glare in his eye hinted an obsessed, ruthless greed for power. He wanted all or nothing. An anxious desire and unquenching thirst for a high station in life drove him to expect perfection in himself and those around him at all times. This frightened Anne a little, but when he held Anne softly and laughed with her, sharing their secret feelings, hopes and dreams, he held her heart captive.

"Marco, I want you too, but I want to be someone special in life also. I don't want to be your shadow and live only in your dreams. I have some of my own dreams too. I wish they were as clear as yours, but they're not. They are hazy and not quite within my grasp yet. Sometimes I feel anxious because I can't figure out what is missing in my life or what purpose my life has. I know there is something out there for me, I just haven't been able to figure it all out yet."

"Anne, you don't need to do anything but love me. I'll take care of you for the rest of our lives. Just say you'll marry me."

Anne fidgeted nervously. How can I marry you or anyone when I don't even know who I am or what I want to do with my life? Anne thought uncomfortably.

"Marco, I'm not ready for that kind of a commitment."

"Anne, I'll never let you go. I love you," Marco said with conviction.

Anne looked at Marco's deep set eyes for a long, awkward moment wishing she possessed his strength and confidence. His hands slid down the sides of her neck and across her shoulders lightly caressing every inch of her tense flesh. He lifted her chin to stare at her troubled face.

The warm glow in his eyes, and his gentle hand gliding on her skin removed the wrinkled lines of tension in her forehead and melted the knots in her muscles into desire. Dormant emotions tingled in her flesh as tides of passion flowed like the raging sea. His eyes, glinting in satisfaction, roamed her face allowing hot flames of colorful sensations to permeate his body. Anne closed her eyes letting his firm tender hands caress and cradle her.

"Anne," he softly breathed, "I love you."

The next few years slid from passion, excitement, flaming ecstasy and exhilaration into agitation, resentment and turmoil. Anne and Marco's plight was at a stalemate. Marco, now accepted into law school, was like a race car driver clutching with a white-knuckled impenetrable grip to the steering wheel of his vehicle with obsessed tunnel vision to the power, glamour, and success waiting at the finish line.

Despite their conflicting attitudes about their priorities, Anne still felt warm in their relationship and was committed to Marco. She deliberately and soothingly rubbed her hand across her bulging stomach with baby oil. She stretched letting the hot July sun penetrate her skin with comforting warmth. A faint smile traced her lips, but a worried look glazed over her eyes. She felt her baby's movements with delight.

How different this felt from the last time she was pregnant. She already felt a strong bond of love between herself and this child. She vowed to give this child enough love to somehow make up for the love she couldn't have for her son. She intuitively knew it was a little girl. "Vanessa," she whispered softly. "Vanessa sounds like smooth, shining velvet. Yes, you'll be my sweet, soft Vanessa," she said closing her eyes, breathing in the warmth of the sun.

Marco's aggressive tendencies to dictate, and Anne's stubborn streak wedged a wall between them. The flicker of disappointment on his face when she was less than perfect clawed at her like sharp fingernails scraping a chalkboard. His jealousy flattered her at first but with time became degrading.

Both of their quick tempers flamed in heated arguments that held no answers to their problems. Anne felt his unflinching ambition meant more to him than she did, and Marco felt her stubborn drive for her own selfish desires outweighed her responsibilities as a wife. Both, anxiously still in love with one another, felt trapped and doomed in a impliable situation.

A few weeks before their baby was due, Marco announced plans to move to another state. He planned to attend a law school far superior to the one he now attended. He disregarded Anne's love for Austin, and the thrill she felt when her mother, Nina and Robert moved there. Her plan for them to all be together again had finally materialized. There was little chance she would let anything separate them again.

"Please, Marco," she pleaded. "Please don't ask this of me." She resentfully felt like a child again begging her father not to leave. She shook her head slightly, biting her lip. Fear darker than words flooded her body. She shuddered and instinctfully filled in the remaining gaps in the wall she started to erect between them.

She promised herself she would not be vulnerable to desertion again but found herself being tossed aside for Marco's career. Slamming the door to her heart, she shut and locked the key in a safe and secure part of her mind. She swallowed hard and fought her burning tears. It was at that moment she knew any hope for their future together was lost forever.

"Anne, you knew how I felt about my career before we married. That has always been perfectly clear. You need to grow up and realize that is the most important thing in the world. I am going with or without you," Marco spit out in anger.

Outraged by being second place to his self-proclaimed mission in life, she lashed out. "I am going to have your child in a few weeks, Marco! I am not leaving my home. If you had one ounce of decency in you, you'd at least wait until I have this baby before you leave."

A plastic smile froze on his face. "I don't have to be there until the end of August, Anne. The baby is due the week before. Maybe by then you'll get some sense into that thick head of yours. I love you now, and I always will, but you have to change your ways if this marriage stands a chance in hell." He turned toward the door angrily slamming it behind him.

Two weeks later in, spite of Anne and Marco's deadlock, Vanessa decided she was ready for the world.

Sweat poured from Anne's brow as she slowly exhaled. Marco held her hand softly coaching her through the next contraction. "You're the most beautiful creature I have ever seen, Anne. I love you," he reassured her as she groaned with another pain. Torment overwhelmed him. He loved Anne like he would never love another but was bitterly frustrated with her attitude. Why does she have to be so stubborn? he regretfully thought.

Anne's mind swam to her last delivery. How different it is to have someone you love with you. She smiled, "I love you too, Marco," she said sadly knowing his decision to change law schools would change their world forever.

"It's time to push, Anne," the doctor instructed.

Anne's beet-red face pulsated with purple veins swelling at her temples. All other sounds grew faint as she concentrated on the tiny life trying to come out of her. This time she wasn't afraid. She attended classes to teach her how to breathe and handle labor and delivery. She was ready and anxious to hold her precious baby in her arms. She felt the head brim and pushed with every ounce of strength in her.

"It's a girl!" Marco yelled in excited pleasure. "She's as beautiful as her mother," he added softly placing her in Anne's arms. They both fiercely held on to one another and the baby. They laughed and cried together, overjoyed with this precious little life and in dreaded fear of what their future would hold.

Chapter Three

SACRAMENTO 1970

Richard stayed in foster care for the next three months until the paper work was finalized. He fought hard to survive. Jake and Marsha were delighted with his determination to recover, and the positive, happy attitude he displayed. The degree of damage to his brain seemed slight, however, he was still too young to speculate. Long black waves of hair fell against his olive skin. Large brown eyes offset his strong, prominent nose. His voice and grip were sturdy, and his smile melted hearts.

"What a handsome young man you're going to be, Richard," Marsha softly said, kissing his forehead. "God sent you especially to me, little one. I'll always love you."

The next two years flew by as Richard grew stronger. His neurological tests encouraged Marsha. However, she grew concerned with Jake's increasingly long hours away from home and subtle hints of emotional withdrawal. She hoped it was a phase that would pass.

Richard was the apple of his sister, Jessica's eye. She loved everything about him. "Come on, Ricky, you can do it," Jessica urged. Her steady unflinching eyes smiled at him with the warm clarity of autumn rain. Tenderly picking Ricky up, she pursed her lip with determination and tossed him a loving grin. He clasped his tiny hand around Jessica's finger. She gently stood him up cautiously guiding him forward.

"That's good, Ricky. Soon you'll be walking all by yourself like a big boy," her voice sang. The smooth curve of her delicate eyebrows arched slightly, and her face brightened. Ricky looked in Jessica's reassuring eyes with open excitement and trust.

Marsha entered the room; her eyes fondly moistened with pride. Jessica's affection and infinite patience with Ricky amazed her. She flashed a tender look at Jessica flitting across the room.

"Mom, he took three steps," she squealed reveling in their accomplishment. Her wide smile displayed open satisfaction with her cleverness and pride in her brother.

A hint of amusement flickered on Marsha's face. "Before long you'll have him running the marathon." She chuckled placing her finger lightly on Jessica's proud chin. She tried to hide her concern for the slight delay in Ricky's muscular development. She hoped her love, Jessica's persistence, and Ricky's strong will would overcome any disability he might have to endure.

AUSTIN 1973

Marco's plans to leave the state were altered by a mistake in his communication with the University. He left Anne and traveled to New York only to find out he would not be accepted there for another year. Although he came home to salvage their relationship, Anne couldn't rise above her anxiety and translation of his actions as desertion to achieve his goals. As a defense mechanism, Anne closed her heart to him in every way.

Their relationship deteriorated at a rapid pace. They struggled over the next seven years on again and off again. They found their transition and divorce painful and confusing. Eventually Anne and Marco both remarried adding more tension and introducing new difficulties to their relationship.

Anne became fiercely overprotective of Vanessa trying to shield her from all the hurts and rejection she suffered as a child. She found it difficult to trust Marco and to accept his changing attitudes. Marco's increasing anger and frustration of Anne's suspicions lead to escalating battles. Neither one could understand how they ended up this way or how to change it. Time passed with no resolution.

After she finished reading Vanessa's favorite story to her before bed, she reached down and gave her daughter a big squeeze. "You know, sweetheart, I love you more than life itself." She looked into her sweet, delicately shaped face.

Vanessa's thick, velvet hair cascaded around her shoulders past her waist. Her serene expression and the warm darkness in her eyes reflected the calm serenity of an early morning. Her flawless coffee cream complexion glowed in the golden moonlight shining through her window. "I love you too, Mommy."

Anne lightly closed the door to Vanessa's room and thanked God for such a lovely child. She turned to her new husband and smiled.

"I thank God for you too, honey. You have been a ray of sunshine in my life. I sometimes am afraid to go to sleep at night because I might wake up and find you were just a wonderful dream."

Jeremy tenderly swept her into his arms. He deliberately moved his lips toward hers, pressing his mouth against her full, wet lips. He touched her lips at first with feathery light strokes then moved his lips down the side of her neck to her firm breasts with slow deliberation. His fingers caressed her tight, smooth stomach muscles rubbing deep into her flesh. Passion pulsed through him. Gently pressing her legs apart, he slid his broad chest and muscular thighs firmly over her body randomly kissing her moist flesh. Their eager movements melted their bodies together in perfect rhythm until their fierce intensity of pleasure exploded.

"Never let me go," she whispered in a sigh softly nuzzling her head on his tight muscular chest.

Sensations of warmth and passion lingered softly into the night. They held each other in a silent, warm embrace. Their bond of intimacy made Anne ache to feel the same breath as Jeremy. Her body settled comfortably into his as they peacefully fell asleep in each other's arms.

Anne, happy in her new life with Jeremy, regretted the hard feelings between her and Marco. Over the next few years, they continued to verbally crucify one another, each for their own self-righteous reasons. Their vile words bit like snakes and poisoned like vipers leaving a chill of an icy winter snow between them. Both yearned to repress their destructive behavior but found themselves in one court battle after the other.

After their divorce, Anne struggled and worked herself through college to become a teacher. She did triumph over all obstacles but regretted the tedious hours she could not be with her daughter. She realized those precious hours lost could never be regained. She was grateful, however, she had her mother and her aunt and uncle. She always knew Vanessa was in loving hands.

Marco's efforts were also victorious. Success avalanched his law career. However, he became increasingly embittered with Anne and so engrossed in his new life, he had little time or energy left to be a parent.

Anne sadly wondered if their success was worth the high price they had to pay? She missed the good times with Marco and his friendship. More importantly, she worried about the price their daughter was paying and wondered how much more she would have to pay.

Anne watched Vanessa retreat a little more into herself each time there was open fire with Marco. Vanessa's sparkling brown eyes saddened into a dark smoky tint of quiet withdrawal while the battles continued. Vanessa skillfully constructed a glazed film resembling shattered fragments of broken glass to cloak her inner turmoil. Her deceptive veil of transparent calmness disturbed Anne. She feared what she read through her daughter's cloaked eyes. The imperious mask Vanessa carefully painted on her face prompted Anne to rearrange her priorities.

Frightened of the consequences for her daughter's well-being, Anne silently declared a truce. She resolved to let the battle with Marco vanish like smoke after a forest fire. She stifled her occasional tendencies to slither back into the same destructive pattern. With deliberate determination, she stepped out of the game of hate shutting the door behind her. She prayed God would forgive her for all the irreversible damage already done. Then she focused on her daughter, her career, and her family decidedly leaving the battle with Marco as a part of her past.

Marco, however, still smelled the stench of the burned forest and was unable to forgive Anne or forget the pain.

Winter gingerly cascaded in. The December rain lightly drizzled and shimmered on the plants in the front yard. Succulent leaves flickered colors of the rainbow through the light coat of rain softly dancing on their leaves. The hint of dampness in the air smelled cool and refreshing bringing life to the surrounding vegetation.

Anne stirred the chicken cacciatore she made for dinner, inhaled the aroma of the sauce, put the lid back on, then walked toward the living room. Jeremy sat beside Vanessa helping her with her math homework. Her face reflected the comfortable feeling she had with Jeremy. She threw back her head and laughed as he joked with her in his usual quiet way.

"Dinner is ready you two," Anne interrupted.

"Oh no!" Jeremy teased, "We wanted to do more homework.

I guess we'll just have to tear ourselves away to eat dinner," he teased dropping his head and protruding his lower lip.

Vanessa giggled, and Jeremy jumped up to give Anne a squeeze.

"It smells scrumptious, just like your mother, doesn't it?"

"It sure does. Mom did you make rice or potatoes with the chicken?"

"All those who want rice put up your hand," Anne tested. They both quickly put up their hands. Rice was one of Jeremy and Vanessa's dishes. Anne could make it every night, and they would be happy.

"Well, you're both in luck. It just happens I guessed right and made rice with it."

"Oh, Mom, you must have ESP."

"Just when it comes to you two," she chuckled.

They all sat in their usual spots and bowed their heads.

"Vanessa do you want to say grace tonight?" Anne asked.

"Okay. Bless this house, Oh Lord, and thank you for everything we have-and each other. And thank you for letting us have rice tonight."

"Amen," they all chanted.

"Vanessa, after dinner I'd like you to try your dance outfit on. You are performing tomorrow, and I want to make sure it looks right."

"Are you getting excited about the performance yet?" Jeremy asked. "I hear there are going to be a lot of people there."

"I am a little nervous, but we've practiced the routine so much, I think it will be all right. Are you going to bring the video camera?"

"Of course we are. You know we wouldn't miss getting our little pumpkin on video, would we?" Jeremy smiled. His green eyes twinkled, and the dimple in his left cheek widened.

After they finished the meal and cleaned up, Vanessa tried on her yellow outfit and performed solo for her mom and Jeremy. She bowed graciously after the performance with a glint of pride in her eyes.

Clapping and whistling they yelled for an encore. Vanessa

giggled gladly giving them the encore they begged for. "Honey, you're going to do just great tomorrow. You look gorgeous in your outfit, and your performance is perfect." Anne hugged Vanessa primping the skirt to her outfit. "Well, I think we all better hit the sack, so we can get an early start.

"I love you sweetheart," Anne said kissing her daughter good night.

The performance the next day went well. Vanessa did as beautifully as her parents predicted. Anne sat there with pride while Jeremy took videos of every move Vanessa made. Anne was amazed at her daughter's graceful, precise movements. Her slender frame glided into sweeping steps. Her shining long black hair, pulled high on her head in a ponytail tied with a yellow bow, flowed through the air. She reminded Anne of an elegant dove soaring through the sky with succinct panther-like grace and precision. How she wished Marco could set aside his anger to share moments like these with Vanessa.

They went out for ice cream after the performance then decided to watch a movie in the evening to wind down after the exciting day. Vanessa fell asleep cuddled between Jeremy and her mom. Jeremy swept her up and tiptoed with her in his arms to her room. He quietly kissed her forehead and tucked her in pulling the sheets up to her chin.

The weeks quickly glided into months. Spring burst forth with blossoms of pink, yellow and lilac. The sun peeked through the few clouds in the sky promising a clear warm day. Jeremy, in his tight jeans and tee shirt, flashed a smile. His rolled up sleeves gripped the bulging muscles in his arms accenting his lean, well-muscled flesh. He looked at Vanessa with wild mischief in his eyes.

"Whoa!" Jeremy yelled as Vanessa dunked the ball in the basket. "We better look out, Anne, or she'll be the next basketball pro of the century."

Jeremy's bronzed skin highlighted his light, wavy brown hair. His perfectly shaped mustache and piercing green eyes, sensually perfected his striking angular face and square chin.

He turned heads wherever they went. Jeremy's never noticed the glances, though. His eyes were always fixed on Anne.

Anne gasped for breath while Jeremy and Vanessa fought for the ball. Both were in top condition and loved the conquest of making the basket. Anne, although in good shape herself, could barely keep up with them. Putting her hand to her chest, she sank to her knees laughing. She watched them quickly dribble the ball eyeing one another with determination to win.

Hearing Anne laughing, they both broke their concentration. They ran over to her tickling her until she begged for mercy.

"I'll do anything. Please stop," she gasped in short breaths inhaling with laughter.

"Let me see...We'll stop only if you promise to make spaghetti tonight," they teased.

"Any...Anything," she stuttered, red from laughter.

Jeremy and Vanessa agreed spaghetti sounded perfect after the long game. They were all famished.

Anne got up, put her hands on her hips, and tilted her head. A smile pursed her lips, and her face brightened. "Last one home's a rotten egg," she yelled turning her head to glance back over her shoulder as she got a head start. She heard their hurried footsteps gaining quickly on her, so she sped her pace to reach the door first. They jerked the door open then fell on the floor panting with exhaustion.

"I'll tell you what," Jeremy announced catching his breath, "instead of spaghetti, how does ordering a pizza sound to you?"

"Now that's a perfect suggestion from my brilliant husband," agreed Anne putting her arm around his waist. Laughing, she lifting her head for a kiss. They decided to order their usual double cheese pizza with thick crust and extra sauce.

"This is a perfect end to great day," Jeremy smiled winking at the two beautiful women in his life.

The next few months were filled with Vanessa's dance recitals, gymnastics meets, and as summer approached, Anne, Vanessa and Jeremy spent every spare moment in the pool. During the evenings they played cards or board games together or sat by the pool talking.

"Anne, next week is our third anniversary," Jeremy stated as they sat by the pool alone. "Do you think dinner and dancing sound good?"

"Anything would be fine. I can hardly believe three years have gone by already. When I was a little girl I never dreamed I could be so happy."

Jeremy rubbed Anne's shoulders while they overlooked the sparkling pool. The stars that night held a brilliant excellence of gold glistening throughout the sky in thousands of flaming pockets.

"I can remember when I was about to start first grade," Jeremy recalled. "My fear of going to school without her for the first time disgusted my mother. She warned me not to get labeled a coward. She told me strong boys weren't afraid of anything and if I showed the other kids I was afraid, they'd all make fun of me. The next day I stiffened my shoulders and fought back my tears. My knees trembled, but I dared not let anyone know I was afraid. I can remember the tight churning in my stomach and the embarrassment of my fear.

"My mother's a good woman. I believe she thought she was doing the right thing. In her own way, I think she was trying to protect me.

"By the time I was in the sixth grade, I began to think what my mother said was true. I started using my strength to cover up my soft side and hide my emotions. That behavior attracted the kind of friends who made me feel emotions and sensitivity were a sign of weakness in a man. I never want Vanessa to feel that way. I want her to be able to express her feelings, no matter what they are, and know we will love her."

"Vanessa will always be open with her feelings to you. I've never seen her so open and responsive to anyone as much as she is with you, except for my mother. Vanessa and Mom sure are kindred spirits, aren't they?"

Jeremy agreed. They both chuckled thinking of Marie and Vanessa's special relationship. "I know you had it rough because your father deserted you, but you sure are lucky Marie is such a great mom. Don't get me wrong, my mother loved all of us and was good to us. I don't think I ever saw her and my dad fight. She just had a different perception of strength in a man, and I wanted her to be proud of me.

"At first, the trouble I got in and the fights that evolved were to prove to my mother I was tough. Then I began liking the respect I got for being strong, and my impulsive anger escalated. The anger I sometimes show now is a direct result of that, but I am working hard to overcome it because of you and Vanessa."

Anne stroked his thick hair and leaned her head on his chest. "Jeremy, I can count on my hands the times we've argued. It is true, though, the fire in your eyes I see when we do argue scares me. It's like your ability to reason and control your actions vanish. Our first big argument was the worst, but you've kept your promise to work on your anger, and I believe you have succeeded. And you've never lost your temper with Vanessa."

"Anne, I love Vanessa. I'll do anything to give her a good life. You two are my family. Speaking of family, why don't we invite your family for dinner some time soon."

"Okay. That sounds great. I'll make homemade ravioli and ask Mom to make her sauce. Nobody makes sauce as good as Mom."

"Stop, you're making me hungry," Jeremy jokingly whined. He was thankful Marie was such a loving grandmother. He knew his mother would not offer the love and support Marie did to his stepdaughter.

Marie, still as feisty as ever, adored her granddaughter. Vanessa and Marie's relationship was more than just a granddaughter and grandmother. They laughed at the same things, cried at the same things, and felt linked through their hearts and minds. They enjoyed each other's company as best friends, and respected one another's feelings with mutual trust and understanding.

Marie came a long way since her husband left her helpless and alone. When she moved to Austin she applied for a janitorial job at a prestigious department store because she was afraid she was too old to get a good waitress job. The man who interviewed Marie felt her outgoing personality should be put to its full potential. He hired Marie as a sales clerk instead of the janitorial position she applied for and within the year she was top sales lady in the department store. Her fellow co-workers as well as the clientele fell in love with her honest, forthright personality. Although she was busy with work and her social life with her many friends, she always reserved special times for Anne and Vanessa.

Anne shook her head. Her thoughts quickly drew back to her excitement about the dinner plans. She looked forward to seeing everyone.

"I'm making you *hungry*," Anne exclaimed standing before Jeremy. Deliberately, she unbuttoned the front of her shirt slowly. "I hope you're hungry for me," she said tossing off her shirt. With a teasing glint in her eye, she lowered herself in his arms.

Jeremy growled and playfully bit her lower lip. He stroked Anne's hair wisping in the light breeze with rich tones of sparkling gold and honey. He gently took her face into his hands. His eyes smiled and searched through the dark satin of her eyes. They burst into her soul with the warm glow of love and passion. The fresh soft dew of ivory on her cheeks flushed in rosy pink under his admiring gaze. She felt his eyes not only reached but caressed the inner depths of her soul.

"Anne, I'll love you till the end of time. I believe our love is so powerful it will even transcend death."

Anne breathed in the delicate smells of the night and the scents of her precious love, Jeremy. The intensity of allowing her body and her mind join with his so completely enabled her to understand how a man and woman could become one. She shuddered wishing this moment could last forever.

The next week Anne invited her family for dinner. Marie made her famous sauce for Anne's ravioli. Robert made his gourmet salad, and Nina brought dessert.

"Aunt Anne," Samuel asked excitedly, "Can we go swimming after we have our pie?"

"Of course you can, but it would be a good idea to wait

about an hour for your food to settle. Okay?"

"Yea, we get to go swimming, we get to go swimming," he sang skipping about the room.

"If you want to go swimming, you better settle down, Samuel," his mother gently cautioned.

Vanessa was the only grandchild until Nina had her son Samuel. After five years of marriage, Nina and her husband planned to have a child. When Nina was six months pregnant, her husband left her for another woman. Devastated by her husband's decision but powerless to change it, Nina moved in with Anne until the baby was a year old, then moved into her own place. In the year Nina lived with Anne, their relationship and friendship grew even stronger.

Anne also formed a special bond with Samuel as she watched him grow within Nina and coached Nina through her delivery. Samuel's uncanny ability to vividly express himself at an early age, and his affectionate nature, gentleness, and enthusiasm for life warmed a special place in Anne's heart.

Her mind drifted. She sadly wondered if the son she gave away was anything like little Samuel. Then, she quickly jerked her hand to brush away the tear escaping down her cheek before anyone noticed.

"I'm with you, Samuel. I need to get in that pool and work off some of that pasta." She laughed overtly rubbing her stomach, pulling at her pants to stretch more room for the food. What do you say if we wait till after we swim to have dessert?"

"I have a better idea," Robert teased, "let's have dessert before *and* after we swim!"

The decision was unanimous. Everyone agreed Robert's idea was ingenious, but no one had enough room in their stomach to actually go through with it. They all splashed and played in the water while Nina took videos.

Marie posed for the camera as Esther Williams on the diving board, and Robert teased Vanessa with his usual antics before they went in to eat Nina's award winning pie. They all pitched in to clean up, played a quick game of cards, and kissed each other good night.

Anne went to work the next day feeling especially happy about the good time she had with her family the night before.

"Anne, there's a telephone call for you."

"Could you possibly take a message?" Anne politely asked.

"I'm sorry, but he said it is important that he talks with you now."

Anne went to the phone wondering what could be so important that it couldn't wait until later.

"Anne, this is your next door neighbor, Lonnie," he stammered.

Lonnie—Anne thought in surprise. Lonnie was a kind neighbor who lived a couple of doors down. She couldn't imagine why he would call her at work.

"Anne, I'm sorry to be the one to have to tell you this," he stammered, "I was on my way to work this morning, and I witnessed a terrible accident." His voice broke off shaking.

"Lonnie, why are you calling to tell me this? What has happened?" she questioned with growing alarm and foreboding anticipation of what words may lie ahead.

"It's Jeremy. He's been hurt bad. They are not sure if he is going to make it to the hospital. You'd better get there quick."

"Oh, my God—No," she stammered.

"Anne—I'm sorry. If there's anything I can do..."

"Lonnie, there is," Anne interrupted. "Please call Darla and have her pick Vanessa up from school. Ask her to keep her until I can get home. Tell her I'll call as soon as I can...And, Lonnie, please tell Darla not to say anything to Vanessa until I get a chance to talk to her myself. I need to be the one to tell her."

"Sure, Anne. I'm sorry," Lonnie's voice broke off shaking.

"I know. Thanks, Lonnie. I'll talk to you later," Anne's voice drifted off.

She looked around the room not knowing quite what to do. Everything seemed to be moving in slow motion. The room began to swirl into a mist of gray fading into black. She caught herself on the desk. She hung the phone up with terrifying numbness in her limbs. A dull ache in her head began to thug as if splintering the bones of her skull and stopping the flow of blood to her heart. In frenzied silence, she walked slowly trying to combat the water consuming her knees with weakness. As she digested the savage stroke of reality, she had an overwhelming need to scream. All she could manage to do was summon a tiny voice from her throat to ask someone to please help her get to the hospital.

On the way to the hospital, time suspended into a cloud of vagueness. She stared straight ahead limp, speechless, and expressionless in dreaded fear there would be no escape to the new dimension her life was about to take.

Her legs took her through the hallway of the Emergency Room toward Jeremy. The doctor briefed Anne brushing away any hope of life ever being the same for Jeremy. She couldn't believe this was happening to them. She felt as if her body belonged to someone else. Speechless, she continued to stare at the doctor acting as though she understood all he was saying.

"There has been severe damage to Jeremy's brain. He is experiencing paralysis on his left side and some speech and memory disorder. His right thumb has been cut off, incapacitating the use of either hand at this time. We could refer you to a surgeon to repair his thumb and partial use of his right hand; however, because of his critical condition, I'd advise you to wait on that decision."

The doctor's mechanical voice droned in monotone syllables as if in rhythm to a metronome slowly ticking away. His eyes barely met Anne's.

When she finally had a chance to speak, she blurted, "Are you saying Jeremy might not live, so you don't want to waste your time on a hand surgeon?" her voice prodded in a panic and irritation. I must sound like an idiot, she thought. Why am I arguing about his hand when he's in there fighting for his life? God, I can't think straight, she thought irritated with herself.

"I'm saying his condition is too critical at this time to do more than hope he gets through the night. We need to take one step a time. I'm sorry."

"I want to see him right now," she insisted with a cold icy glare appalled by the bleak picture the doctor painted.

She set aside the sickening words pounding in her brain and followed the doctor to Jeremy. Acutely aware she must put on a brave front for Jeremy, she cloaked her fear and stepped into the room.

"Hi, sweetheart," she said in a soft voice gliding her fingers across the back of his hand.

Jeremy's face was as pale as the gauze band wrapped around his head. His shiny green eyes clouded into a flat, hollow gray. He tried to muster a smile but squeezed his eyes shut for a moment. The corners of his mouth twitched nervously. He tried to prevent his tears from streaming down his face. Unable to stop the flow of water from his eyes, he gazed at Anne like a lost child and bit his lip. His face screamed in agony and confusion.

Anne's stomach convulsed and twisted but she tried to mask her terror. She protectively stroked his hair and softly told him to rest.

She sat with him in breathless anxiety. Through the next week, she randomly kissed the tears cascading down his soft skin while he thrashed about in agony.

In the flash of a moment, a slip of fate jolted her existence into a black hole. She sat in rigid fury cursing the disastrous turn of events. She prayed for God to save them from this desperate, ugly situation.

"I know I've prayed for a lot of things in my life, God. But this is just too much to bear. How can this have happened and *why*?" she whispered.

"It just isn't fair. Why does life have to be so damned painful? Everything was so good with Jeremy," she thought squeezing her eyes shut. "Please, God—do something to fix this. *Where are you? I can't feel you !*" she screamed under her breath.

She slumped over Jeremy's bed with frustrated exhaustion—angry and afraid.

Vanessa stayed the first night with Anne's friend and neighbor, Darla. She was glad Marie was going to move in temporarily to help. She really needed her grandmother now. She felt Marie was the only one who would understand her pain and her fear.

Anne's friends, neighbors, and family helped all they could to alleviate additional stress on Anne. She felt overwhelmed by their kindness and support. They all tried to ease Vanessa and Anne's pain but knew nothing could turn back the clock to their happier days with Jeremy. Their strength and kindness carried her through the days and months that followed.

Light pressed through the curtain of the room when the doctor entered.

"You made it through a very rough week, Jeremy. Do you know who you are?"

"My name is Jeremy."

"That's good, Jeremy. Do you know what city you live in?"

Jeremy's eyes searched Anne's for a hint to help him answer the question. Then he slowly lowered his head and shook it like a child.

"That's all right, Jeremy. You are in Austin."

"Tell me, Jeremy, can you feel this?" he questioned while he poked and pinched Jeremy's leg. Jeremy shook his head again staring at his leg. Tears brimmed his eyes. The doctor smiled at Jeremy and patted his shoulder. He then turned to Anne.

"Anne, since Jeremy is now out of critical danger, we are going to send him up to the seventh floor for rehabilitation for about a month."

"What happens after that, doctor," Anne asked flatly.

"Well, we'll have to see how he's doing at that point. Each brain-injured person responds differently. There are specific symptoms that are consistent with different areas of the brain that are injured; however, each symptom can vary from patient to patient, and they may exhibit all or some of the deficiencies in various extremes.

"The prefrontal and posterior part of Jeremy's frontal lobe

are damaged, and there is acute unilateral damage to the cerebellum. The frontal lobe controls voluntary muscle control. The prefrontal lobe synthesizes abstract thought and controls emotions. Memories are stored diffusely throughout the brain, but more complex memory patterns are located in the temporal lobe and is believed to be transmitted to the prefrontal lobe where they are synthesized into complex patterns and form the basis for abstract thought.

"The prefrontal areas also receive many associate fibers from the thalamus, a center concerned with emotions. The cerebellum regulates muscle tone of posture and equilibrium and smooth performance of voluntary and muscular groups.

"In other words a person has a tendency to fall sideways and has difficulty with quickness and accuracy of his limbs. Jeremy's inability to use his left side, his severe depression, partial memory loss, and loss of balance are all a direct result of the injury to these areas of his brain. Jeremy needs rehabilitation to facilitate other brain areas to help him function on a higher level than he is now."

Her arms dropped stiffly to her sides with clenched fists. She felt her fingernails cutting into the palm of her hand and tried to loosen her grip. Fatigue clouded her thoughts. Her eyes locked on Jeremy's limp left side.

"His left side does not respond to any stimulation, the gangrene that settled into his right hand is delaying surgery for another week, he has large gaps in his long term memory, and his short-term memory is inconsistent. His paralysis and memory dysfunction render him paraplegic, unable to feed himself, brush his own teeth, or even use the bathroom unassisted. His mental capacity is that of a ten year old severely depressed, suicidal young boy, and you're telling me he is out of critical condition and ready for rehabilitation!" she spit, amazed at the vast amount of medical jargon she picked up in the last week.

"Anne, we do not think he is in high risk of losing his life now. This floor is only for those who are in critical danger of dying. The other problems Jeremy is experiencing need to be attended to on the rehabilitation floor," he said with a polite smile.

Anne wanted to slap the fake pasty grin from his face but knew none of this was really his fault. Instead, she silently walked beside her husband as the attendants wheeled him up to the seventh floor.

When they reached the seventh floor, a shrill desperate cry jerked Anne's head to a woman in a wheelchair. A large iron apparatus attached screws into her head. Her wild eyes and lips were all she was able to move. She repeatedly shrieked the same sounds over and over. Unable to form any syllables with her tongue, the same inaudible sound gushed from her lips in an eerie owl-like screech.

Oh, shit, Anne thought. I never did like hospitals. I don't know if I can handle this.

The halls and rooms seethed with pathetic people forced to live as shells of human beings after some hideous mishap yanked away the promise of a normal life. Anne continued to walk down the hall. Then suddenly, a young man in his early twenties plunged at her. His face held a crazed expression of fear and confusion. He approached her yelling something about the acid he last took. Anne learned later he suffered from recurrent relapses of his last bad trip on drugs and alcohol. Two hospital attendants took his arms and safely led him back to his room.

The wild look of horror on the man's face coupled with the woman's hideous screeches sickened Anne. She put her hand to her mouth and bolted to the nearest restroom. She choked as the little lunch she managed to eat that day burned its way up her throat into the toilet. She laid across the toilet while sobs jerked her body. Her breath continued to heave in short heavy gasps in her chest.

Exhausted and weak, she feebly tried to pull herself out of her hopeless despair. She threw water on her face and slurped water from her hands to gargle. She fumbled in her purse for a piece of gum to take the rank taste in her mouth away. She then plodded back to Jeremy's room. She felt she was sinking in a filthy pool of murky water with weights attached to her body and no way out.

Tossing a cautious glance into Jeremy's room, she quickly scanned the faces of the three other patients. Her heart felt heavy as she sadly observed their pain. She tried not to stare at the nineteen-year-old boy who suffered a stroke and had been in a coma for six months. His head protruded like a turtle out of his shrinking, frail, and limp body. There was no sign of life on his still face, and his hair looked glued to the sides of his head. His parents visited him daily. They never gave up hope for their son. They looked at Anne when she passed giving her a reassuring warm smile.

Later, Anne grew to admire these two courageous people for their continued support and kindness toward everyone. They fought the battle with their son for many years. He never recovered.

The second bed held a middle-aged man who fell off his roof. He nodded to Anne when he caught her gaze. A cast covered most of his body. His legs were extended and hanging from some contraption resembling a torture chamber. Anne couldn't imagine how he could sleep entrapped in that position. There seemed to be nowhere she could look without seeing unbelievable pain and agony.

The third bed tore into Anne's heart with overwhelming sympathy mixed with anger. A seven-year-old boy laid there in his own excrement waiting for the nurse to change his soiled bed. A drunken truck driver changed this boy's life in a blink of an eye crushing most of the bones in his tiny body. It turned out the driver had previous offenses driving while intoxicated.

The stench traveled across the room clinging to the inner hairs of Anne's nostrils. Anne tried to ignore the smell and drown out the sound of his tiny desolate voice whimpering in pain. When the nurses carefully began to clean him up, his haunting brown eyes bulged sadly from his shaven head pleading with them not to hurt him anymore.

A heavy sense of pain reeked through the still, thick air of the dimly lit room. Anne felt her stomach slither again but had no more food in it to throw up. She flirted with the idea of grabbing Jeremy out of his bed and running with him in her arms to a place where there was no more pain—no more sadness.

Her mind carried her into a fantasy. A white Pegasus with large shining wings swooped down to save them. Briskly flying away, he carried them out of this nightmare into safety through a bright, glittering rainbow.

Angered by the absurdity of her thoughts and futile attempt to escape reality, she shook her head and quickly walked over to Jeremy. Her fingertips brushed over his clammy palms trying to soothe the look of fear in his panic-stricken face.

The next three weeks slid from hopeless expectations to the bleak realization that Jeremy's legs and mind were never going to be the same. The physical therapists helped Jeremy use a walker to drag his left side and taught Anne how to massage his limp limbs. For the most part, Jeremy sat in his wheelchair gazing ahead with alternate looks of festering anger, frustration, and depression.

After he was released from the hospital, therapy continued enabling Jeremy to walk with a cane and eventually on his own for short periods of time, but Jeremy slipped further into himself as the years lingered on.

"Anne, honey, you've got to start taking care of yourself," Marie urged with worry. "You need to eat, Anne. You need to keep up your strength. You're not going to do anybody any good if you end up in the hospital."

"I know, Mom, but when I think about eating I just get this huge lump in my throat. My stomach seems to tighten and shut down."

Anne's eyes were framed with dark circles. Her complexion yellowed, and her body shrunk to a skeletal eighty-five pounds during the two years following the accident. Disjointed, restless nights were filled with tossing and jerking about only to awaken to the same hideous nightmare.

During the first year of therapy, Anne learned how to manipulate Jeremy's legs three times daily to prevent his firm muscles from withering into weak frail limbs. Jeremy learned how to manage most of his own personal hygiene and how to feed himself. These simple tasks became remarkable feats since the series of unsuccessful operations on his right thumb rendered him unable to grasp. Regaining only a limited use of his left hand complicated simple movements even more. Anne struggled to have enough energy for both herself and Jeremy. But her strength slowly seeped out of her body turning her passion for life into a life of passionate denial, confusion, and exhaustion.

Jeremy worked the right side of his body pumping it into a powerful mass. With Anne's help, his left side looked normal but only functioned enough to get around for short periods before tiring. Darkness engulfed him, though, as he sunk deeper into an uncontrollable, angry depression.

Anne felt herself changing. She lost her lust for life. She lost her assertive, spunky attitude. She lost her ability to laugh. She withdrew to detach herself from the pain. Her driving force was to help Jeremy through this. She lost all sense of self.

Their evenings spent at the pool now were filled with sobs of hostile anguish and despair. It replaced their previous laughter and excited expectations of sharing their hopes and dreams while growing old together. Jeremy's periodic loss of control over his dark, violent side increasingly consumed his personality with each episode withering his will to live. He frequently sat in a dark corner of the bedroom with the door locked huddled in a tiny ball. He tried to control his depression but sobs racked his body and violent urges seeped into his mind.

"Anne, you have to go live with your mother for awhile. I need some time alone to work through things."

"What can you work through without me that you can't work through with me here to help you?" Anne argued.

"I can't explain it, Anne. Just look at what's going on here. Why are you fighting me on this? You are only making things worse. If you love me, you'll give me some time alone." He delicately touched Anne's black eye, her bruised cheek and swollen lip.

"I did this to you, Anne," he cried, softly stroking her face. Anne lowered her eyes dejectedly. She knew he was right. It was the only time Jeremy lost all control. She explained away her bruises as an accident to hide her embarrassment and perceived failure to avoid the situation. So far he had only hurt her, he hadn't hurt Vanessa, she rationalized. But what if he lost control with her little girl? She had no right to put Vanessa in this kind of jeopardy. She struggled to make some sense out of what was happening to her world.

"I don't understand why you don't know how empty my world would be without you," Anne cried.

"Anne, I'm begging you to go. Please go."

"All right, Jeremy, I'll go for awhile, but only if you promise to continue therapy and hire someone to take care of you while I'm gone."

The next day she packed her things. She drove with Vanessa to her mother's in a daze.

"Mom, why isn't Jeremy coming with us?" I'll do anything if he would just come with us. Please Mom, tell him I'll do anything."

"Honey, you know both Jeremy and I love you very much," her voice shook, "but this is the best thing for us right now. I'm sorry, sweetheart."

Anne sensed the same strange quietness in Vanessa that frightened her before. She prayed she would know how to help Vanessa through this confusing time. Jeremy used to always know the right thing to say to make Vanessa feel better when she was down. How Anne wished she could come up with some magic words to use as a Band-Aid to fix the explosion that shattered their world.

During the next month, Jeremy quit taking Anne's calls and eventually had his number changed. The only communication he allowed was through letters. His letters were written as though two distinct personalities were expressing their thoughts. He claimed undying love in one sentence and a violent, irrepressible urge to have Anne killed in the next sentence. The one side of his mind twisted into believing Anne was responsible for his disability and depression. He believed if she were dead, he would be cured. The other side of his mind loved Anne with a protective, nurturing, tender passion trying to protect her from everything—even himself. Anne's fear of the mingled love-hate battle obsessing Jeremy's mind left her feeling helplessly out of control and alone.

While reading one of Jeremy's letters she heard a knock. She set it aside and walked slowly to the door.

"Are you Anne Edwards?" the strange man inquired.

"Yes, I am."

"This is for you." He handed Anne an envelope and walked away.

As she read the contents, Anne's eyes grew wide. She clenched her teeth grinding them from side to side. Her lips turned blue and quivered. Her face soaked with tears, and her knuckles turned white from the tight grip she held on the paper. She brought her hands up to her face. Holding her head in her hands, she slumped over crying in loud jerking sobs.

"Anne, honey, what's wrong?" her mother rushed over.

Anne handed Marie the papers demanding a dissolution of her marriage.

This is happening too fast. How can this be true, she thought in panic. She bolted to the bedroom throwing herself across the bed. Her body convulsed involuntarily with torment wracking her mind through the night.

The morning didn't look rosier. It didn't hold any promise of salvaging her marriage or picking up the pieces of her life. She tried to imagine life without Jeremy, but couldn't. Yet, she knew there was nothing she could do to change things. During the next few months she unsuccessfully pleaded with Jeremy through her letters not to go through with the divorce action.

She felt like a miserable failure. Despondency mixed with a dead, hollow feeling crept into her heart. She cursed the brutal current of wretched circumstances that savagely played havoc with her destiny.

Chapter Four

Sacramento 1981

Marsha walked down the hall into Ricky's room to wake him up for his first day of school. She thought of the changes in her life that occurred since she first adopted Ricky. She had such high hopes for a neat life wrapped in pink paper neatly tied with white satin ribbon and a large beautiful bow. She tried to analyze the cold distance between her and Jake that began to slowly unravel her dreams. Her mind drifted back to the day Jake left. Marsha felt Jake's overbearing demands for attention and perfection were unrealistic. He's acquired an irritable lack of sensitivity for anyone but himself, Marsha thought. She found herself spending more time with the kids and less time with Jake.

"Marsha, We both know I'm just not happy living here

anymore. I'm sorry things have turned out this way—but they have. I don't know exactly when I began to enjoy my time away from home more than I do being here. I truly am sorry. I have found my happiness elsewhere, though, and I think it's better for all of us if I leave," Jake sadly said while he packed his bags.

"Jake, I love you, but I can't understand the way you've changed. Most of all, I can't believe your attitude towards Ricky. Why can't you accept him the way he is? It tears me apart to feel the distance between us and the wedge between the two of you. It seems no matter how hard we try, it just isn't enough for you."

Marsha stood with her head high trying not to show how her insides were crumbling into small fragmented pieces. She searched her husband's handsome face but found only a cold glare. She knew there was no way to save their marriage or to smooth over Jake's relationship with Ricky. The strain between them became increasingly more evident through the years. His expectations for a son were not met with this child, and his appetite for other women proved stronger than his love for her.

He longed to retrieve his feelings of love and commitment, but the harder he tried, the further away he felt. Although they both believed their marriage would last forever, the cold reality of its finality slammed shut as Jake closed his suitcase and left.

"Ricky—it's time to get up for school," Marsha said lightly touching the soft, thick black mass of waves on his head.

Ricky didn't usually wake up this early, so Marsha had to try several times before his eyes focused on her. He tossed his head from side to side, rubbing his eyes with his fist, then groaned realizing he had to get up for school. School was not his favorite place to go. The warmth of his bed felt too good to have to leave so early in the morning.

The intensity of his beautiful, dark, Italian eyes sometimes took Marsha's breath away. She smiled into them as she patted his hand.

"Boy, I wish it was summer, and we could still be on vacation. Mom, can we go to Disneyland again and Six Flags, too?"

"You really enjoy that, don't you, Ricky?"

How she enjoyed the summers with the kids. They traveled the states enjoying the beauty of Mt. Rushmore, Yellowstone, and Oregon. She relished the look in her children's eyes riding the roller coasters and sharing the spectacular views of the Grand Canyon.

"Come on, sweetheart, how about a nice bowl of cereal before you get dressed?" Marsha said pulling back the covers and helping Ricky out of bed and into his slippers.

She wished Ricky would enjoy school as much. Marsha hoped this year would be better than last year. Ricky was now in fifth grade. His behavior in school each year got worse. His short attention span and temper kept Marsha busy with the teachers and counselors. She wished they would encourage his strong points instead of dwelling on his weaknesses. She did believe, however, that he would connect better with this year's teacher and hoped for the best.

He excelled in math and displayed a keen interest in sports, but he was high strung and began to experience involuntary twitches in his face and head. The right side of his upper lip twitched up, and the left side of his lower lip twitched down intermittently.

Ricky's sensitivity and embarrassment turned into hot anger when teased by the children. He learned to use his temper as intimidation to stop the teasing. In spite of the rough exterior he displayed, his insides trembled, and he wanted to shrink into a tiny ball and hide when a tremor took hold of his face contorting it against his will.

"Hi, Sis," Ricky smiled at his sister, Jessica, when he entered the room for his breakfast. Although they were seven years apart, Ricky looked up to and considered Jessica his dearest friend. He called her "Sis" from the time he began to talk. In fact, it was one of his first words. He rarely called her by her name. His eyes always lit up when he talked with his sister, and he spent as much time around her as he could.

"Hi, Ricky," smiled Jessica. "I'll be ready to go at 7:30. Make sure you're ready by then. Okay?" Jessica brimmed with pride as she jiggled her new car keys. She got her driver's license over the summer and saved the money for her first car. She bought a cute used powder blue compact car, so she could afford the gas and insurance. Marsha surprised her and paid for the first year's insurance for her birthday. She used her extra money to fix the car up just the way she wanted it.

She promised Ricky he wouldn't have to take the bus to school anymore. She was especially happy about that because of the previous trouble Ricky had with fights on the school bus. It tore her up when kids made him uncomfortable about his disorder.

Ricky was recently diagnosed with Tourettes syndrome, a widely misunderstood neurological multiple tic disorder. It is characterized by involuntary, rapid, repetitive movements of functionally related muscle groups. It affects the eyes, face, head shoulders, limbs, trunk, and sometimes involuntary patterns of speech occur. In Ricky's case, he experienced twitches in his head and face that contorted his mouth and jerked his head.

Marsha took him to a neurologist when his tics began. She called the adoption agency to report the problem. At that time, she strongly pointed out she loved her son. She intended not only to keep him but to get the medical help he needed to get relief.

The medication prescribed helped but did not dissipate his involuntary tremors. Marsha learned that Tourettes occurs when a defective gene interferes with the release of a neurotransmitter called dopamine, which helps regulate motor control. The nervous system of those with TS have excessive amounts of dopamine. Doctors still don't know exactly what causes Tourettes syndrome, and there is no cure for this mysterious brain dysfunction.

Children have a hard time paying attention which leads to discipline problems in the classroom unless the teacher is appropriately equipped to understand and work with a child with this syndrome. Jessica felt her brother was misunderstood. She knew the gentle, loving side of her brother and blamed the fights with the other kids on their teasing and cruelty.

She tried to encourage Ricky to ignore it but knew her little brother couldn't. For the most part, Ricky cherished his relationship with his sister and would do anything to please her, but he couldn't control his temper when someone made fun of him—not even for Jessica. His slight frame usually took the worst side of the fights he was in, but that didn't stop his temper from exploding either.

Jessica gave her brother's shoulder a loving squeeze after she found his assigned room. She wanted to hug and kiss him but knew it would embarrass him at this age. She smiled and told him she loved him then watched him enter the room. He turned around when he found his seat and gave Jessica a big smile and waved. She hoped his new teacher would recognize and encourage his abilities in math and art and his creativity with cartoon characters and unique designs.

Jessica looked at her watch and headed for her car, so she would make it on time. She drove to school and parked by her friend, Monica's car.

"Hi Jess!" Monica called from her car inhaling a joint. "Do you want a hit?" she said trying to keep the smoke in her lungs as long as possible.

"Okay. Just one. We need to hurry, or we'll be late for class." She quickly inhaled one hit then another and scurried off to her english class. Since Jessica met Monica a few months ago, she began starting each day sharing a joint with her friend and finding parties on the weekends to drink and get high. Her pleasant, bubbly personality matched her pixie face, and her large wide smile glistened with the twinkle in her bright blue eyes.

Although she had many friends and liked to party, laugh, and feel wild and free, so far she didn't let her good times interfere with her work or her schooling. She only had a year to graduate, and she didn't want anything to screw it up. She knew her mother had worked too hard to provide a nice life for her and her brother. She wanted Marsha to be proud of her. However, before she realized it, an occasional joint and an occasional party had turned into a joint every day, and a party every weekend.

Oh well, she thought as she ran to class giggling. I can handle it. I just over did the partying a little this summer. Now that school is in, I can cut it back some. I just needed a couple of hits this morning to take the edge off the first day back to school. The bell rang just as she entered the classroom. She hoped the teacher couldn't pick up the scent of the marijuana. She glanced quickly around the room. Sitting in a vacant seat as far away from the teacher as she could find, she fumbled in her purse for a piece of gum to hide any marijuana scent that might be on her breath.

AUSTIN 1984-88

Lost in her thoughts, Anne sat at the table staring straight ahead. Nina walked in the house with a confident stride. "Hey, little sister. You need to find something to wear tonight. We're all going out to the Robin's Roost to have a little fun. Three girls from work and Jill, and Donna are going," she informed Anne flashing a big smile.

"Nina, please, I'm really not in the mood for fun."

"I know. That's just my point." She placed her hands on Anne's shoulders and looked squarely into her face. "So what do you plan to do, Anne, feel sorry for yourself for the rest of your life?"

"I don't know." Anne cast her eyes down. "Maybe I will."

"Well then I mistook you for someone else I used to know. Someone else that was full of spunk and pride."

"Oh, Nina, what ever happened to that girl? I can't seem to find her." Anne grimly stated.

"She's sitting right here, honey. She just needs a little help from a friend. Come on, let's find something for you to wear."

Nina's face reddened in blotches trying to hide her tears.

She hugged her sister and scurried her into the bedroom to change her clothes for a night out on the town.

Anne, determined to have a miserable evening, exchanged unpleasantries with the doorman and found fault with just about everything. She sat at the table lost in her own thoughts, wishing she had stayed home. Feeling claustrophobic with all of the sounds and laughter, she headed for the restroom. She needed a moment of silence. Plowing up the steps through the crowd disgusted with the atmosphere of lonely hearts, alcohol, and heavy cigarette smoke, she decided to call it an early evening.

"This is not what I call having a good time," she grumbled to herself under her breath. How could I let Nina talk me into this, she thought with irritation. I'm going to pull my hair out of my head if I don't get some peace and quiet soon.

"Anne…is that you?"

Anne's head jerked up toward the familiar voice into the smiling face of an old friend she used to date.

"Derek. Talk about a ghost from the past. I'm surprised you recognized me after all these years." She searched his blazing steel blue eyes and wondered how the years treated him since she'd seen him last.

"I'd know those big brown eyes anywhere. You're looking good Anne," he deceptively flattered her. The Anne he used to know was a voluptuous exciting girl. She held a hint of wild adventure in her eyes and bubble that sparked her personality with a flair of laughter. Now her gaunt face and sullen eyes emitted a hollow, haunting sadness. Yet, deep in her eyes he could sense a faint glimpse of the girl he used to know.

Anne suddenly remembered that was one of the things she liked about Derek. His suave manner with women, his flirtatious flattering, and his blatant charm made women feel sensuously beautiful.

"How are you Anne?" he asked with genuine concern.

"I'm terrible. I'm going through a divorce I do not want, and I'm miserable," she readily admitted.

Derek admired Anne's open attitude. Too many of the women he ran across these days put up facades hiding behind too much makeup and jewelry. He felt their callous attitudes toward men and bitterness over undesirable circumstances in their lives took its toll on their physical appearances. He thought it also hindered their willingness to be open in new relationships. He found honesty a rare quality.

"Anne, I know what that's like. I've been there myself. My wife left me for another man last year. It was one of the worst years of my life. I'm just beginning to recover from it. It's not easy when you lose someone you thought you were going to spend the rest of your life with."

Derek's face exhibited knowledge of how deep Anne felt her pain. It was comforting to talk with someone who seemed to understand. The crowd around them seemed to disappear. They exchanged stories of their failed marriages, caught up with gossip of some old mutual friends, and chatted about their careers.

"Do you have any children, Derek?"

"No, I raised my ex-wife's daughter from another marriage, but I never had one of my own. How's your daughter? She must be pretty big by now."

"Vanessa's doing just fine. She's almost a teenager now. I can't believe how quickly she has grown up."

"Well, if she's half as beautiful as her mother, she must be a knock-out." Derek reached into his pocket and pulled out a card handing it to Anne. "I was just on my way out, Anne, but here's my card if you want to give me a call sometime," he offered.

"Better yet, why don't you give me your number," he suggested, sensing Anne's pride would prevent her from calling. "If nothing else, it looks like you could use a friend."

Anne wrote her number down for Derek with mixed feelings, thinking he probably wouldn't call anyway.

"It was nice to see you, Anne. I'll call you."

"Okay, Derek, good-bye."

Anne went back to the table after she used the restroom and explained who the good looking, tall man on the stairs was. The girls at the table delighted in the gossip.

"See, Anne. I told you it was a good night to go out," Nina bragged.

"Well, we'll just have to see if he even calls," Anne doubtfully stated.

The rest of the evening was the usual girl talk with intermittent dancing. Anne, grateful to get home in the quietness of her room and relax, wondered what Jeremy was doing tonight.

The next morning she awakened to the sound of the phone ringing. She rolled over and picked up the phone with her eyes still half-closed.

"Hello, Anne? This is Derek. I just called to say good morning, and that I am glad we ran into each other last night."

"Thanks, Derek, so am I," Anne said surprised he called so soon.

"Anne, what are you doing tonight?"

"Tonight?" she questioned, thinking he was moving a little fast.

"Yes, tonight. I thought you might like to come over for a barbecue," he chirped.

"It depends if my mother can watch Vanessa tonight. She's old enough now that she really doesn't need a sitter, but I don't like leaving her alone."

"I'll have dinner ready at 7:00. Call me back if you can't make it. I live just past the intersection of Fair Oaks and Lindsey Drive. Do you know where that is?"

"Yes, I don't live far from there myself."

"Good. You make a left on Fair Oaks. The third street down is Lindsey Drive, make another left. I'm the fourth house on the left-hand side."

"That sounds pretty easy to find. Unless you hear otherwise, I'll see you at 7:00."

"Great, I'll see you then, Anne."

Anne hung up the phone in disbelief. Whatever was she thinking? She was still a married woman. The divorce papers weren't final yet. She fidgeted nervously wondering if she should call him back and break the date. What is he expecting from me anyway? she wondered. I'm not the same girl he knew so many years ago.

This will never work. She picked up the phone to cancel the date, then put it back down. What would it hurt to go and renew an old friendship? I'll tell him straight out that friendship is all that will come of this. I'm still in love with my husband, and I'm not ready for anything else right now.

Vanessa popped her head in the room to let Anne know she was ready for school.

"Hi, honey, I'll be ready to take you to school in five minutes," Anne said jumping out of bed quickly throwing on a pair of jeans and a shirt. She glanced in the mirror and shrugged. I look as shitty as I feel, she thought, carelessly tossing a brush through her hair. That's good enough, I'll take a nice hot shower when I come home. Hell, maybe I'll even treat myself to a bubble bath. She ran out of the door grabbing her purse and brought Vanessa to school.

Anne spent a luxurious hour soaking in a hot tub filled with the bath oil her friend, Maggie, gave her for a gift. She rubbed her hand over her legs amazed at how silky and smooth they felt. She put a towel around her then walked over to the phone.

"Hello, Maggie, this is Anne. Thanks for the bath oil. I can't believe how soft my skin feels. Maybe I should rub it on my face to get rid of some of the tiny lines starting to pop up," she laughed. Maggie was one of Anne's closest friends. She could be herself and confide in Maggie without fear of rejection or judgment. "Listen, Mag—I met a man last night I used to date years ago. He asked me to his house for dinner tonight. What do you think?"

"Anne, I think you're crazy if you don't go. You need to start relaxing and enjoy yourself a little. I think you'll have a good time."

"Do you really? What about Jeremy? I'm so confused about my life, Mag."

"Listen, Anne, who wouldn't be confused with all you've been through. Just go over and have a good time. Don't make yourself all nervous about it."

"Yeah, I think you're right," Anne said slowly. Hey, Mag, thanks for the advice. I'll call you tomorrow and fill you in on how it went."

"All right. Bye, Anne." Maggie hung up and grinned. It was the first time in a long time she heard a hint of excitement in Anne's voice.

Dinner that night went great. Anne and Derek comfortably slid back into their friendship as though no years had ever separated them. Anne stayed until two in the morning. They had dinner, confided in one another, gave each other advice and encouragement, and played a game of Scrabble. Anne loved playing games, but Scrabble was her forté. She rarely lost a game. Nina and Vanessa always put up a great battle, but Anne's luck with the game was hard to beat. Derek made a formidable opponent, but Anne quietly smiled when she put her ten point letter on a triple word score and won the game.

Derek rolled his eyes up toward the ceiling and patted his chest. "I almost had you, Anne, but that last killer word did me in," he teased.

"Derek, I hate to win and run," she said with a twinkle in her grin, "but I better get home and sleep real fast. I have to get up in six hours."

Derek walked Anne to the door and gave her one soft kiss before she left.

"I'll call you tomorrow, Anne. I'm glad you came over."

Anne looked up at his shining dark blonde hair, gentle blue eyes and soft full lips. There was a feeling of honesty between them that she liked.

"That sounds good, Derek. Bye."

Anne drove home feeling oddly secure with the comfortable feeling she had with Derek that night. She was too tired, though, to try to make sense of it all. She just hoped God would guide her in the right path because she was too confused to make any decisions on her own right now.

Anne and Derek spent every night the next week either talking on the phone or with one another. Anne told Vanessa about Derek and was surprised at her reaction. Vanessa didn't seem to like the idea of Anne spending so much time with him.

At dinner Anne smiled warmly at Vanessa. "Honey, I'd like you to meet Derek on Saturday night."

"What about Jeremy, Mom? How do you think he'd feel if he knew about this?" she questioned in a cool, irritated voice.

"Look, honey, Jeremy doesn't want me in his life anymore. I've got to go on without him."

"He's just mixed up right now. He'll change his mind. You'll see." Vanessa swiftly turned and abruptly stalked away.

That week Vanessa's and Anne's relationship felt strained and awkward. Any time Anne tried to mention Derek, Vanessa changed the subject. Anne had hoped Vanessa's feelings would soften by Saturday night but feared they wouldn't. She sadly understood the confusion Vanessa must be feeling with the abrupt changes in her life.

Vanessa stayed focused on how much she loved Jeremy. She felt Anne's going out with Derek was a blatant display of betrayal to Jeremy and their life together as a family. She didn't understand why she had to meet Derek on Saturday. What is the point, she thought. He doesn't mean anything to me anyway.

Anne was unaware of the extent Vanessa's bitter feelings. She knew Vanessa cherished the times with her Grandmother and did not realize Vanessa felt lonely and abandoned when she spent time away from home to be with Derek.

As the week wore on, Anne and Vanessa remained in a stalemate. Saturday night approached with tension still in the air. Anne answered the door with a smile to greet Derek. She then called Vanessa out of her room.

"Vanessa, this is Derek."

"Hello, Vanessa. I've heard a lot about you," Derek said extending his hand to Vanessa.

"Hi," she flatly said, not returning the gesture. "I'm working on some homework that I'd like to get back to," she dryly commented walking toward her bedroom.

"I'm sorry, Derek. She's been through so much lately.

She's usually very pleasant," Anne explained trying to cover Vanessa's rude behavior.

Derek felt sorry for the position Anne was in but felt uneasy with the sense of fury Vanessa displayed in her rude behavior. He hoped he was overreacting, but his gut told him to be wary of the dark glare he caught in Vanessa's eye. Derek turned his thoughts to Anne.

"Well, gorgeous, I hope you're hungry because we have reservations at fabulous Chinese restaurant in town."

"That sounds good to me, and I am famished," Anne said grabbing a sweater and opening the front door. A cool slight breeze wisped across her cheek wiping away the heavy feeling she had in the house with Vanessa. She wasn't quite sure how to handle things, but knew she needed to have a heart-to-heart talk with her daughter very soon.

The next morning Vanessa came out of her room with a sullen look on her face. She tried to avoid conversation with Anne, but Anne pressured her into talking and confronted her about her behavior toward Derek.

"Vanessa, why were you so short with Derek? He is a very nice man."

"I don't like him," Vanessa spat. "I want to be with Jeremy. I still love him, even if you don't. Why are you wasting your time with this weird guy. He'll never love you like Jeremy does. You and Jeremy belong together—we all belong together," she yelled, storming into the bedroom, loudly slamming the door behind her.

Stunned by her daughter's opinion and reaction, Anne wasn't sure how to deal with her odd behavior. Anne didn't approve of Vanessa's behavior, but her heart went out to her daughter's pain and loss.

She went into Vanessa's room and sat on the bed. "You know, honey, you'll always be the most important person in my life. No matter who else I am with, our love is something very different and special. Nothing can ever compare to the love a mother has for her child."

Anne flinched thinking of the child she gave away and hoped

the mother he lived with loved him as much as she did Vanessa. She believed her son was with someone who loved and cared for him more than she was able, but the thought of giving away her own flesh and blood left her feeling degraded and unclean.

When Vanessa was a little girl, Anne told her she previously had a baby who died in childbirth. She wanted Vanessa to know about her brother but didn't have the courage to tell her the real truth. Anne, being a staunch proponent of honesty, hated this horrible lie. Not only did she feel she had to lie to her daughter, but she felt had to lie to the whole world. She shuddered. Her mind jolted back to Vanessa aware of how confused she must feel.

"I love you, honey," she softly reassured Vanessa looking straight into her sad eyes. "It's all right to still love Jeremy. I know he still loves you too. I wish I could explain what's happening, Vanessa, but I don't understand much of it myself. She kissed Vanessa goodnight feeling the icy chill of Vanessa's cold glare burning in her back as she left the room.

Over the next few months Derek provided support and understanding when Anne felt low. But as Derek and Anne grew closer, Vanessa drifted further away.

Derek and Anne sat on the floor holding hands in front of the fireplace with their heads leaning back on the couch. The last few months together with Anne was a welcome relief to his loneliness. In spite of the turmoil in her life, he still felt warm and comfortable with her. He placed his hand under her chin and stole a kiss.

"Derek, you know the thing I love the most about our relationship is our ability to be candid about our feelings. I've been doing alot of thinking lately. You know I've grown close to you, but I need you to understand that at any time before the divorce is final, if Jeremy changes his mind, I still want to salvage my marriage."

Derek's sea blue eyes stared at Anne in disbelief. "Where is this coming from, Anne? How can you say that with all the time we've spent together lately?"

The gentle blue in his eyes turned from the soft current of a soothing ocean into a ramble of foaming waves crashing angrily against the shore. His stomach rumbled and tightened. A dark wave of confusion and anger set in. He struggled to see things from Anne's point of view but felt she wasn't being rational. He was too much in love with her now to accept losing her. He shuddered to think how he'd recover from another loss.

"Anne, you need to close the door on that relationship," he flatly stated. "You aren't thinking clearly. With me you can laugh and enjoy a normal life. All Jeremy has to offer is more pain and turmoil.

"You can't turn back the clock, Anne. Things will never be the same between you and Jeremy again. If you try to live in the past, it will dry you up and swallow you into a dark void hole. It's all right to reminisce once in awhile. It's good to look to the future and plan. But you have to live in the present if you want to survive. I love you, Anne. I believe you love me too. You need to let him go."

"I'm sorry Derek, but it's just not that easy. I want to let him go, but he is still a part of me. I can't give up until I know there is no hope at all. Even then I don't know if I can. I don't want to hurt you, Derek. My feelings for you are too strong not to be completely honest with you. I just want to be sure you know exactly where I stand," she said as kindly as possible.

Derek took Anne home early that evening. He was furious with her. Her words tore into his heart like a knife. How can she be so stupid? I know her feelings for me are strong. We could have such a good life together.

This stinks, he angrily thought. How did I ever get myself mixed up in this crazy situation? He reached into the cabinet for a bottle of bourbon and poured a couple of shots into a glass of Seven-Up. He drank it down in two big gulps reaching for the bottle again.

Anne laid in bed tossing in confusion. Derek's right, but I still am Jeremy's wife. Please, God, she prayed, the Bible says You will only give a person as much as they can handle.

Well, this is just more than I can handle. I'm tired, Lord. You've got to take me out of this limbo and show me what to do. I need strength and peace. Throughout the night she lashed about unable to calm herself down enough to sleep.

A few months later the opportunity to turn back closed like a steel trap snapping shut around a defenseless animal trapped in the woods. Her divorce was final. There were no more choices to be made. She knew she had to tear that part of her past out of her mind. She had to set herself free. Just as an animal trapped in a treacherous grip of steel teeth biting into her flesh has to gnaw off her own ripped, bloodied limb to set herself free hoping she'll survive.

She wondered why the determination for survival dominated her awareness that complete recovery was impossible. Peace of mind and spirit became a remote, far-fetched improbability. She had to concentrate on the slim chance of survival in spite of the absurdity of another chance for happiness, or even contentment. She knew she had to stop living in the past, or she would die—and for some strange reason, she was not yet ready to die.

Her mind bolted to Vanessa, and her lips tightened with dread at the prospect of confronting Vanessa with the news. She inhaled walking toward Vanessa's room.

"Vanessa, I want to talk with you," she said lightly tapping on the door.

"What about?" Vanessa queried suspiciously.

Anne realized beating around the bush would make matters worse, so she came straight to the point.

"Honey, the divorce was finalized today."

"So what is that supposed to mean? I guess you're saying you and Derek can live happily ever after now. Well, maybe you can, but I can't."

Anne looked at Vanessa strangely. She couldn't believe her reaction. She knew Vanessa would not take the news well, but she did not expect such a hateful response.

Vanessa stormed out of the house and ran to her best

friend, Melissa's, house. She cried and cursed the world. Shit, she thought as she rang Melissa's doorbell. Nobody cares about the way I feel.

"Hi Melissa," she said stifling her tears.

"Hi, Vanessa. Come on in. You look terrible. What's wrong?"

"Melissa what am I going to do?" she blurted. "My Mom's divorce is final today. I can't believe she let this happen! I feel like nobody wants me in their life anymore.

"My father only sees me when he absolutely has to. When we do see each other, we never have any time alone together. Either his wife or other kids are always there. I love his other kids, but he doesn't understand that I need some special time with him. He always criticizes me anyway, and we usually end up in an argument before I leave. Let's face it, he cares about his job and everything else more than me.

"I know my dad's relatives love me, but when I see them I can't communicate because their first language is Italian, and they speak very little English. If we could understand each other better, I know they'd help me—especially my grandfather, I know he's always praying for me. And my grandmother's so sweet. I love to hear the sound of her voice even if I can't understand what she is saying. It's useless, though. I know I'll never learn Italian.

"I know my mom loves me, but she doesn't care anything about my feelings. She keeps seeing Derek even though she knows how I feel.

"And Jeremy has never called me—not once! I'm never going to be able to see him again. I miss him, Melissa. What am I going to do?" she sobbed. "The only one that cares anything about me that I can talk to is my grandma. What would I do without her?" she stuttered in anguish.

"I care about you too," Melissa said, putting her arms around Vanessa and letting her cry.

During the next year Anne and Derek struggled through their differences. Although they were still having a hard time with Vanessa and adjusting to one another, they decided to get married. It was a small, quiet wedding with only Anne and Derek's immediate families and a few close friends. Both Anne and Derek were committed to making a happy home life for Vanessa, not realizing the road blocks they would have to face.

Derek wanted to give Anne and Vanessa stability and prove to them that life can be more gentle than the rocky road they had just been down. Derek wanted to bring normality back to them and peace back into their hearts. How he wished the past didn't cling onto them so tightly. He believed, with time, he could wipe out the ugly face of his own painful divorce, as well as their tragic loss. There was no way anyone would know just how deep Jeremy's knife would tear into their new family.

A week after the wedding Derek sat in the living room and heard the phone ring. Anne picked it up in the other room, so he continued reading the paper.

"Hello," Anne smiled.

"Hello, Anne," his voice trembled then trailed off.

"Jeremy is that you?"

"Yes, Anne. I just called to congratulate you. I hope you're happy, Anne."

"Jeremy this isn't the way I wanted it to be..."

"Anne," he interrupted, "I just called to hear your voice and to congratulate you. Nothing else. Please—just talk to me for awhile. How's Vanessa?"

"She misses you terribly, Jeremy. She's still doing good in school and is on the cheerleading squad. You wouldn't believe how she's grown.

"I hear a woman moved in with you. It sounds like you're doing much better. Do you love her?"

"I'm not capable of loving her, Anne. She's just a companion," he said in a flat weak voice. "I don't want to talk about her anyway, I just want to hear about you and Vanessa."

"We are both okay. Jeremy. Is something wrong? You don't sound good. Are you all right?"

"I'll never be all right, Anne. Things with me will never be all right. I just needed to hear your voice."

Anne talked with Jeremy about Vanessa for awhile and listened while he spoke about things in his life. His words were quiet and soft but disjointed and abrupt. His voice held a depressing tone that disturbed Anne.

"It was good talking with you Anne, but I guess I better let you go now. Good-bye."

The phone abruptly clicked. Anne sat trembling. Listening to the dial tone, she wondered what prompted this strange call. Derek finished the article he was reading and went back into the bedroom to check on Anne.

"Anne, honey—what's wrong? Who was that?" he questioned as he took the phone out of her hands and placed it on the receiver.

"It was Jeremy. He said he called to congratulate us, but he sounded very depressed and strange. It gives me an eerie feeling," she said rubbing the tiny bumps on her arms that made her hair stand on end.

Derek took her in his arms and stroked her hair. "It's all right, Anne, I'm here. You know, you need to start placing more trust in the Lord and hand your problems over to him in faith. I know you believe in God, Anne, but since I have found a personal relationship with the Lord, my life has never been the same.

"I believe if you start to study the Word in the Bible and focus on the personal message of love and forgiveness the Lord has, you will begin a journey that will transform your heart and the way you think about everything. The book of John is a good place to start. In the very beginning it says,

> *Through him all things were made, without him nothing was made that has been made. In him was life, and that life was the light of men. The light shines in the darkness, but the darkness has not understood it.*

"God talks about grace. He reminds us of the many blessings we have received because He loves us.

> *He who comes after me has surpassed me because*

he was before me. From the fullness of his grace, we have all received one blessing after another.

"You have to remember you only exist because God made you. He wants you to shine in His light. I know you've been through so much in your life, Anne, but I truly believe the Lord has worked in you to prepare you to walk in His light and to help others with their journey.

"You may have stumbled and fallen in the past, you have made some good choices and some bad ones, but you were never truly alone. You have not only survived all of your trials but have grown because of them." Derek looked into Anne's eyes and saw an eager glint to hear more. "I guess one of my favorite parts is:

For God so loved the world that he gave his one and only Son, that whoever believes in him shall not perish but have eternal life. For God did not send his Son into the world to condemn the world, but to save the world through him.

"Can you imagine how much love that is? That God would allow His Son to feel the agony and pain He suffered here, so that we can spend eternity with Him?"

"Yes, Derek, I do. I believe in God, and I pray to Him all the time."

"I know you do, Anne, but do you get into the Bible and read His word?"

"No, I don't, but I like what you have said to me, Derek. I think I'll start to read more of it."

"Anne, don't stop there. After you finish the book of John read 1 John. It talks about the Word of Life and walking in the Light. It talks about letting go of hatred and turning to love and understanding through the Lord. It says, *The world and its desires pass away, but the man who does the will of God lives forever.* This is God's promise to ETERNAL life. He promises eternal life in exchange for our commitment to love Him more than we love things in this world. All we have to do is love Him and accept him in our hearts as our Savior and Lord. It's a tremendous responsibility once you decide to learn about God's word and change your life.

"God tells us, *'Go and sin no more.'* That is very hard for us because of our human natures. The easy part is surrendering our love of material things for God's love. The hard part is surrendering our own selfish attitudes and desires. All we can do is pray for the strength to keep His word and to live our lives as He would want us to."

Anne smiled at Derek. She felt a stir in her heart realizing she needed to pick up the Bible and begin to read and understand the message in it.

"Just forget about the phone call and think about what I said, okay? Let's get something together for dinner. I'm starved, how about you?"

"I guess you're right," she agreed as Derek guided her toward the kitchen with his arm around her. Anne tried to take her mind off of the strange call, but it continued to pop in and out of her mind all week.

The next week Anne was called out of the class she was teaching into the Principal's office. Derek stood there with a solemn look on his face.

"Derek, has something happened to Vanessa or Mom?" she panicked, wondering what he was doing there in the middle of the day.

"No, honey, they're all right. I do have some bad news though. I got a call from Jeremy's neighbor. He killed himself last night, and he killed the woman he was with. He shot her in the head while she was asleep then turned the gun on himself."

Her fine brows arched in shock. "Oh my God. I can't believe it. I can't deal with this, Derek. How could he do this? Why in God's name did he kill that girl?"

She wrung her hands and paced slowly around the room lost in the sea of memories swirling in her head. The pressure behind Anne's eyes burned into a hot blaze. She clutched Derek's arms for support. The empty stillness in her stomach turned into a hot fist of pain. She closed her eyes and leaned her head forward.

"Please take me to Vanessa," she whispered.

Her mouth became dry. Her tongue felt like cotton wrapped around it, rendering it unable to move. The veins in her slender throat protruded as tears pelted down her cheeks. She clasped her arms around herself and began rocking. That's what the phone call was all about, she quietly thought. He called to say good-bye. Her lips quivered and her teeth began to chatter inside her mouth making her head jolt intermittently from side to side.

"Why didn't he tell me he was going to do this? I know he's thought of it before, but why didn't he reach out for help?" she muttered.

Her mind throbbed racing with questions that would remain unanswered forever. She pictured Jeremy huddled in a corner with a gun. She wondered what was going through his mind before he pulled that trigger.

What were his last dark thoughts? she wondered. How did he feel before he completed his final escape? She pictured his smile. She thought of their last conversation. Could I have said anything that would have stopped him?

Pain tightened its grip on her soul. It festered into a mixture of guilt, remorse, and a gnawing question of why she was not the one who died with Jeremy. Why was an innocent young stranger's life snapped out of this world instead of hers? She wondered how she felt as the bullet tore through her skull ripping her head apart. Her insides convulsed at the thought.

The drive to Vanessa's school seemed like a thousand years. When they drove into the parking lot, Anne silently wiped her red eyes. She prayed for guidance to help her daughter.

Derek called the school, so Vanessa was waiting in the office. "Mom, what's wrong?" Vanessa panicked seeing Anne's face.

Anne's weak, raspy voice tried to break the news gently to Vanessa, but she felt her daughter slip out of her reach as Vanessa jerked her hand up to her face groaning a deep guttural cry of agony. There were no words to comfort her or explain how such a thing could happen.

If only she could have said or done something to stop him from this hideous act. If she was still with him, maybe this wouldn't have happened. Her mind drifted back again to Jeremy huddled in the corner of the bedroom with helpless depression taking over his mind. She knew deep inside if she hadn't left him, she would be the one with the bullet in her head—and more than likely Vanessa would be dead too.

Why, Jeremy, why couldn't you get better? Why did that damn truck have to hit you in the first place? Why was her life filled with so much agony? Do I have a sign printed on my forehead, God? Does it say: Look out, Anne's happy! Something better happen to screw it up? She winced with a hateful, bitter glaze shining through her tears.

That night Vanessa stole the bourbon from home and made plans to spend the night at Melissa's. She was furious with how the circumstances in her mangled life stole away any chance for her happiness. She felt as though misfortune hovered over her like a dark swollen sky before a storm, jolting her life with bolts of lightning. Jeremy's death slammed shut any open window of hope for her happiness. She sobbed with her friend and drank herself dismally into oblivion.

Chapter Five

SACRAMENTO 1984-89

A slit in Jessica's eyes slowly opened then squeezed tightly shut to block the light piercing through the blinds in her window.

"Oh, shit," she murmured bringing her hands up to her head to massage her temples. Her mouth opened and closed a few times trying to suck some moisture out of the air onto her dry tongue. It's been a long time since I felt this hung over and miserable, she thought. Boy am I glad I'm not into that routine anymore.

She slowly dragged her legs to the side of the bed and used both arms to lift herself to the edge. She attempted to stand then sat back down letting the room settle in first.

For a couple of years this was a regular routine of Jessica's.

She got caught up in the drugs, alcohol, and the party syndrome until her life started to make no sense. Then she met Steve. The corners of her eyes wrinkled with a smile. Last night was his bachelor's and her bachelorette party.

The wedding is next week, she thought with excitement. I'm so lucky to have found such a gentle yet strong man. He treats me with respect yet isn't afraid to let his hair down and have fun. His sensuous eyes and sexy dimple in his chin makes his chiseled face soften when he smiles at me. She could almost feel his large, powerful hands smoothly gliding over her body.

"Yes, indeed, Steve, one more week and I'll have you for a lifetime. I'll make you the happiest man in the universe," she said as her feet took their place on the floor to hold her body. She stretched and yawned looking at herself in the full length mirror in front of her. She could see her rounded figure and her ample breasts through her thin white nightgown.

She ran her fingers through her hair, shook her head to fluff her tousled waves, and grinned in the mirror. "One more week," she said then made her way into the shower.

The week flew by with last minute arrangements. Nervous tension accelerated. Smiling, Marsha primped Jessica's full satin gown. The low V-shaped cut trimmed with wide satin bows at the top and near her waist proudly accented her voluptuous figure.

"I don't know who is more nervous, me or you," Marsha joked.

"Mom, don't be nervous. You and Steve get along great, and I'm happier than I ever imagined. I know Steve's parents have far more money than we do, but they are kind people. The more you're around them, the more comfortable you'll feel."

"As long as you're happy, sweetheart, that's all that matters," Marsha said blinking back the moisture in her eyes.

When she walked down the aisle, Jessica's radiant smile lit up the room.

"This is the most beautiful wedding I've ever been to," squealed Marsha's friend, Janice. "Jessica is breathtaking. I'm so happy for her."

The reception, held on the golf course of Steve's parent's home, was exquisite. Everything down to the minute details was elegant. The green rolling hills, the gorgeous display of food, the fresh flowers on the cake, the linen napkins, the elegant centerpieces on the tables, and the music met the occasion with grace and warm sophistication.

Rick stayed close to Jessica. He tugged intermittently on his cummerbund wishing he could slide into a comfortable pair of jeans. Although happy Jessica married such a great guy, he felt he was losing a part of himself. Home would not be the same without Sis. They had been through so much together. She was always there for him and defended him when his father or his step-mother, Belinda, were unreasonable.

He glanced uncomfortably at his father and Belinda across the room. Belinda caught his wistful glance. She stared at him from under her wide-brimmed hat. His shoulders slumped and he turned away. He awkwardly walked behind Jessica with his eyes fixed on her shining smile and her bright eyes trying to shake off Belinda's icy glare.

His eyes started to twitch, and he could feel his facial muscles begin to contort. He kept his head lowered until the spasm subsided then tried to nonchalantly check out the buffet at the food table. His head twisted to look at Jessica again. He smiled with pride that she had gotten herself together and decided to make a good life for herself.

"Hey, Rick—Smile," he heard as the camera flashed. He would be glad when this day was over.

Over the next few years, some of Rick's school friends began to experiment with drugs. Rick didn't have an interest at first, but as time wore on, he decided to try some. He liked the way some of the drugs made him feel happy, relaxed, confident, and energetic. He dabbled with all sorts of mixtures until he found the drug of his choice—crystal methadone amphetamines. He smoked a lot of marijuana, but found the speedy feeling he got with crack and meth a more exhilarated high. He liked the feeling he had on them. He felt he could take on the whole world. In fact, they brought out a curiosity in him and a courage that vibrated his being. Before long he belonged to the drug. By the time he was nineteen, he transformed into someone Marsha hardly recognized.

"Mrs. Tess," Marsha groggily heard as she picked up the phone. She peered at her clock. It read 2:35 A.M.

"Yes. Who is this?"

"This is the police department. Your son, Richard Tess, is in our jail. There will be a bond hearing tomorrow morning at 8:30."

"My God, what did he do?" Marsha's insides quivered. Her heart raced. Her mind blurred with wild frantic thoughts.

"He was caught vandalizing a government building, and he was apparently on drugs."

"Is there any way I can talk to him?" Marsha's voice shook.

"I'm sorry, Ma'am. You'll have to wait until morning."

"All right, officer. I'll be there then."

Marsha couldn't believe her ears. She envisioned her son in jail. Anguish racked her mind. He had previous incidents with drugs, alcohol, and the law, but this sounded like big trouble. She tried to ease her jerking body but knew sleep was out of the question. She got up, made herself decaf coffee, and let the tears blaze down her face. She felt alone and scared.

The next day Marsha advised Rick to use the county defender as she did not have the money to hire an attorney. Rick felt embarrassed by his actions but thought the system made it into a bigger deal than it was.

"I'm sorry to cause all of this trouble, Mom, but I didn't think the sprinkler system we set off would do so much damage."

"That's the trouble, Rick. You didn't think at all. How could you? You were too messed up on drugs. You promised me you'd quit and straighten up after your last DUI ticket."

"I know I did, but it's not that easy. I just wanted to have a little fun."

"Well, I hope it was worth it, son, because I have a feeling you're going to pay a high price for it this time. I love you, honey. I don't know what else to do or say to help you turn your life around.

"Why do you have to be such a rebel? Why can't you stop and think before you do these crazy things?" Marsha wrung her hands as she looked into her son's sad, dark eyes.

"I promise you, Mom—when I get out of here things will be different. You'll see...I love you too," he added.

Marsha wanted to believe Rick but had heard these words too many times before. She sadly got up and went home. Rick was sentenced to four months in jail and a $9,000 fine. Marsha visited him once a week and hoped this lesson would turn his life around once and for all. It was one thing to get into mischief at school. It's another thing when you get mixed up with drugs and were in jail, she thought in dismay.

Jessica visited every week also and showed him pictures of her son C.J. Rick loved C.J. from the moment he was born. Rick used to gently place his hand on Jessica's stomach to feel C.J. moving inside her.

"I wonder how anyone could give up a child after carrying him inside of herself feeling it grow and move like this?" Rick asked with confusion.

"I wonder who I look like, Sis? I look at my face in the mirror, and I wonder if I have her eyes or her hair. I wonder if she ever even thinks about me. Probably not. I guess she has forgotten all about me by now."

"I don't know, honey, but I do know that we love you and thank God every day that you were sent to share our lives with us," Jessica said with love shining through her eyes.

"Are you sure about that? Even with me getting into this trouble?"

"Rick, you're going to be all right. You just need to settle down. I know what it's like to want to have fun. I know it's not easy to change, but you need to think things through before you do them.

"And yes, I still love you very much—no matter what."

"I love you too, Sis," Rick smiled then pointed to his latest creation. "Hey, Sis, I've been doing a lot of drawing in here on these plastic cups. Do you think C.J. would like to have one of them?"

"Rick, these drawings are fantastic. You really have talent. I wish you would pursue it. You know C.J. would love to have one of them."

Rick blushed. "Well, our time is up. I'll see you next week. Okay?"

"You bet, I'll see you then."

I don't know how I'd get through this time if it weren't for Jessica and Mom, Rick thought later.

Thank God I can hear the baseball games in here and draw. I'd go stir crazy if I couldn't. He reminisced about his years of playing soccer and baseball. His mother never missed a game. He smiled and thought about the basketball court in the yard. He played nearly every day with the guys on the block. He rarely lost a game. They'd play some basketball then dive into the pool to cool off. A smile pursed his lips. He thought about the good times he shared with his friends on the block.

When he met Johnny and Linda, he started messing around with drugs. He wished he had never met them. He wondered if he was strong enough to stop seeing them once he got out.

The next four months trickled away slowly. He could barely contain his excitement when Marsha came to take him home. The Federal Building incident cost him his job, so the first thing he needed to do was find work.

A few months later he found a job but was back with Johnny and Linda again snorting and smoking meth.

After one of his late night excursions, Marsha confronted him. "Rick, you're coming in at all hours of the night. It's 3:30 in the morning. This is too hard on me. I get up early to go to work.

"Besides, you look horrible and your attitude is terrible. You don't do anything to help out around here, and when you're home you stay in your room with your stereo blasting. Maybe it's time you got a place of your own."

"Why don't you get off my back? You're always trying to

run my life… I'm sorry, Mom. I didn't mean that. Look, Johnny's been after me to move in with him. I guess this would be a good time."

"You know I love you, Rick, but I think this will be for the best."

When Marsha left, Rick kicked a magazine on the floor and called Johnny.

"Hi, Johnny, it's Rick."

"Hey, man, what's going on?"

"Things aren't going too good at my house. My mom's bugging me to find a place of my own. How about putting me up for a few weeks?"

"Well, you'll have to sleep on the couch, but I guess it will be all right."

"Great, I'll catch up with you sometime later today."

"O.K., Rick, I should be home after 5:00."

"I'll see you then, John, bye."

Rick hung up, rammed his fist into the door, then packed his bags.

The next two weeks at Johnny's was one big party. Rick snorted a line of meth and cranked the music up. The room, filled with smoke, clutter, and people either high on crack or meth, began to close in on Rick. I've got to get some fresh air, he thought. He pushed open the door and walked outside. Linda sat on the porch with her legs crossed and a cigarette in her hand. Her long, straight, blonde hair moved slightly with the breeze.

"Hey, Rick. What's goin on?" she slurred.

"Nothing much. That room was just starting to close in on me."

"Rick, you seem restless lately. You need to relax—here have another hit, and you'll feel better," she said leaning over to expose her breast.

Rick took a hit then brushed the wisp of hair from her forehead kissing her softly. She lifted her arms around his and drew him closer to her. Her mouth searched for his. Her hands caressed his lean tight muscles as they fell back on the grass.

She kissed him deeply and moved her body to match his.

"Rick, let's go upstairs," she breathed with quick gasps. Taking his hand, she led him upstairs into Johnny's room. She slid off her top, pulling him onto the bed. They explored each other's bodies with their hands. His lips moved from her mouth and traveled down her body until she shivered in delight.

The next thing he knew, it was morning. He had only a vague recollection of the night before. He didn't remember how the night ended or notice that Linda took all of his money out of his pants leaving him with only some small change.

"Rick, get up," Johnny said with urgency.

"What's up?" Rick questioned propping himself on his elbow.

"Shit hit the fan last night. The landlord came over this morning and told us we had to get out by the end of the week because of the complaints about the parties and loud music. I'm going to go live with Susan until I can find another place. You need to find someplace quick."

Rick flung his head back on the pillow and stared at the ceiling. Great, he thought. What am I going to do now? Damn, this really pisses me off. He got up and reached for his jeans. He fumbled to get them on then angrily stomped down the stairs.

The next month was a series of sleeping a night here and a night there, trying to just get by. Rick developed a nagging cough from poor eating and sleeping conditions but continued to smoke the meth and not take medication.

The stifling air simmered with blistering waves of heat. The sidewalks sizzled and glowed reflecting the sun's scorching rays. Rick looked up at the murky brown sky. It held a few low heavy clouds filled with fat swelling raindrops. The white hot afternoon smelled of moisture, yet the bright sun pierced heavily through the oppressive sky looming with gray shadows.

It looks like we're in for some heavy rain, Rick thought. Maybe it will give us some relief from this heat. On the other hand, I better make sure I have someplace to sleep tonight. I sure as hell don't want to get caught in the rain. Rick walked up to Linda's apartment with a carnation in hand and knocked on the door.

"Hi, beautiful," he said with a short low chuckle handing her the flower.

"Where have you been for the past week, Rick. A phone call would have been nice," she dryly said reaching for the flower.

"I'm sorry, Linda, but things have been crazy—forgive me?"

She flashed him an irritated look then softened when their eyes met. "Come on in. Do you want something to drink?"

"I'd love a beer, but I'll take whatever you got," he said forcing a smile from his face. He stared vacantly ahead while Linda got him a drink. His mouth trembled. His face remained empty, and the words awkwardly tumbled from his lips.

"Linda, I need a place to stay tonight. Would you mind if I crashed on the floor—just for tonight?"

She hesitated. "Okay, Rick, but I'm low on dope. Can you get some from Johnny?"

"Sure. I'll come by about 6:00," he said finishing his drink.

"I'll see you then, but don't let me down. Make sure you get some good stuff."

Rick plodded out of the door to get to work before the rain came, but the clouds began to indignantly spit a silver sheet of rain pelting relief for the swollen clouds. The rain lashed against his face drenching his clothes as he ran the rest of the way to work.

He held onto his chest for relief trying to take a deep breath. His face glistened with sweat by the time he arrived at Linda's. He stood by the door and thought of his first girlfriend, Karen. How different she was from Linda. She was soft and sensitive. She had the most beautiful eyes he had ever seen. How he wished things had worked out between them.

He shook his shoulders. Quickly, he snorted a hit of meth then knocked on the door. He was glad he managed one more night with a roof over his head and couldn't bring himself to think beyond that.

AUSTIN, TX—1988-1990

Anne walked down the aisle in her black gown and cap. Derek, Marie, and Vanessa proudly waved to her as she stepped forward to receive her master's degree in education. Anne's eyes sprang to life when she looked through the crowd into her family's faces.

"Way to go, Mom," Vanessa proudly called out, excited for her mother.

Vanessa's mind drifted back to the last few years. They had been filled with bickering, hostility, and a house filled with tension. Vanessa felt a stab of guilt as she watched her mom. She knew her actions had been wrong but couldn't seem to stop herself. Acutely aware of the fine line between happiness and loss, she didn't want to let Derek into her heart. She did everything she could to keep him at arm's length.

She spent all the time she could away from the house. When she was home, she stayed in her room. Her smile seemed to die with Jeremy. She resented Derek moving so quickly into their lives and just taking everything over. It was as though Jeremy never existed. Her feelings ranged from constant mild irritation to bitter anger. The only time she felt good was when she was partying with her friends.

The drugs, alcohol, and parties took their toll, though. When she was introduced to cocaine, the real trouble began. She moved out of the house two months before her high school graduation and quickly found herself free-basing coke. She sold or hocked everything she had to keep supplied in the drug.

Anne and Derek fought bitterly over Vanessa, and eventually over just about everything. The unmistakable air of their crumbling marriage and lost dreams weighed heavy on both of them.

Derek began drinking more than usual. Anne took as many classes as she could to keep her mind off her problems and to stay away from the house as much as possible.

Marie believed Anne and Derek were good for one another and did what she could to encourage them. She worried about Anne, though. She felt Anne never fully recovered from her experience with Jeremy. Anne still looked physically and mentally run down. It seemed there was an empty edge to Anne even when she appeared to be smiling.

Just when both Anne and Derek felt there was no hope for them, they decided to try a counselor. Something deep inside of them didn't want to let their relationship die. Something made them cling to each other and ride through the storm. They looked deep into their hearts and changed the things that were pulling their relationship apart. Their determination for a successful marriage began to balance out their many incompatibilities of their opinions and habits.

Vanessa recalled the turning point in her life and in her relationship with Derek. He reached out to her in one of the lowest times and offered his support. The initial fun she felt when she began to do drugs wore off. It was no longer a welcomed escape. Realization set in that the drugs were now controlling her life. She recognized the need to walk away from them. She needed to set her life back on the right course.

Derek and Anne encouraged her to try a twelve-step program to conquer the demon-like, relentless choke-hold that suffocates a drug victim's sense of reason, morality and self-worth. The destructive serpent drowns you in a sea of endless self-mutilation. It ultimately commands painful daily discipline to defeat the monster's grasp. It renders a never-ending uncertain destiny of constant battles with no easy road to victory. With the help of her family and friends,Vanessa started the first step of her journey toward recovery.

Her father also tried to reach out to help her during this time. She still had many unresolved issues with him but they both began to try to salvage their relationship.

Derek approached her and asked if she had a minute to talk. He sat across the table and looked into her eyes.

"I'm so proud of you, Vanessa. I know this hasn't been easy. I just want you to know how glad I am we're finally getting along. I never wanted to be the one to bring pain into your life. I wanted to be the one to make it all better. My parents never fought. They gave me a good life. I wanted it to be that way for us. I wanted a good life for you."

Vanessa felt a pang of sympathy mixed with tenderness as she looked into his eyes. She knew he meant what he was saying and smiled at him for the first time.

Vanessa's thoughts bounced back to Anne's face. Anne threw Vanessa a warm, happy grin. She framed Anne's delicate face in her camera catching the gleam in her mother's eyes. She snapped the picture just as Anne held up her degree in the air.

"Doesn't she look gorgeous," Marie bragged putting her arm around Vanessa. She helped Anne over the years to work through her failing marriage and through Vanessa's problems. Although Marie worried about Vanessa's safety at times, her faith in her never wavered. She knew Vanessa better than anyone. She believed she would eventually pull herself up and rise above her problems.

Christmas rolled around before anyone was ready that year. Anne and Derek not only salvaged their relationship but felt closer than ever. Anne stood at the kitchen table with a speck of flour on her cheek and pans scattered about as she baked her last batch of cookies for the Christmas party.

Her hips swayed to her favorite Dean Martin Christmas music, and she hummed along with him. Derek tiptoed into the kitchen unnoticed behind Anne, put his arms around her waist, and swayed to the music with her. She laughed and turned around on her tiptoes for a kiss. "I decided to bake another batch of chocolate chip cookies for you before the party since they're your favorite."

He spied the stack put aside for him and went for a glass of milk. "I guess I'll just have to eat them for an appetizer before dinner," he said with twinkling eyes.

"I had the feeling that's what you were going to do, so I put aside an extra stack for later," she smiled.

"Ah, you are the love of my life," he grinned. He took a big bite out of the cookie watching Anne's hips continue to sway to the music while she finished baking. Happy they weathered the storm of their shaky marriage and were now on steady ground, he felt warm that he married and opened his heart to his sensitive, bright, and competent lifetime companion.

He took her into his life with expectations of being together forever, but got caught in glorified skewed memories and longing for a more youthful time when he felt he had more control of things. He thought of the verse in Second Timothy.

> *Flee from the evil desires of youth, and pursue righteousness, faith, love, and peace, along with those who call on the Lord out of a pure heart. Don't have anything to do with foolish and stupid arguments, because you know they produce quarrels. The Lord's servant must not quarrel; instead, he must be kind to everyone, able to teach, not resentful. Those who oppose him he must gently instruct, in the hope that God will grant them repentance leading them to a knowledge of the truth, and that they will come to their senses and escape from the trap of the devil, who has taken them captive to do his will...You know all about my teaching, my way of life, my purpose, faith, patience, love, endurance, persecutions, sufferings. Yet the Lord rescued me from all of them.*

Derek believed the Lord rescued his marriage and set them on the right path. He smiled deeply and finished his cookie. He admired the waves curling lazily around Anne's petite, gentle face, the ivory softness of her skin, and the light in her eyes that danced like flames flickering in a warm fireplace. The scorching sun paled in comparison to the warmth he felt at this moment.

Derek believed their marriage started to take root when he and Anne began to trust in the Lord and placed their relationship into His hands. He thought of the verse in the Bible he and Anne read together before they began counseling.

> *Again, I tell you that if two of you on earth agree about anything you ask for, it will be done for you by my Father in heaven. For where two or three come together in my name, there am I with them.*

They prayed God's will to be done in their marriage and

trusted in the Lord. Anne and Derek both prayed with firm commitment and resolution to work together and pray together for their marriage.

Derek glanced at the plaque of Jesus opening a door Marie had given them last Christmas. He grinned and said out loud, "Ask and it will be given to you; seek and you will find; knock and the door will be opened to you. For everyone who asks receives; he who seeks finds; and to him who knocks, the door will be opened...Therefore everyone who hears these words and puts them into practice is like a wise man who built his house on the rock."

Derek believed his house finally had its foundation on the rock with the Lord watching over them.

Saturday rolled around. Anne walked out of the bedroom wearing a red chiffon flowing skirt and matching blouse. She looked around the room pleased with the decorations and the food she had prepared. A smile pursed her lips. She thought of the long way she had come since that frightened, angry little girl in the alley. She wondered what path Evan's life had taken and smiled remembering the first time she sat in his beautiful car and how nervous she was.

Since then Anne discovered unique things in herself she was unaware existed. Her study, her work, her spirituality, and her values became increasingly more important to her as time went by. She shed the bitterness of the past and followed the lighted path to her present and to her future. For the first time in her life, she felt at ease and secure. She believed Derek's and her trust in the Lord was the hand that came down to save them and to prepare them for their lifetime journey together.

She thought about Marco and Jeremy. Her thoughts then drifted to the women in her prayer group. She was thankful for her friends and their decision to get together every other week to join in prayer and thanksgiving for the Lord. They believed prayer was essential for their school, the children, the teachers, the parents, and their community. The small group of women sang songs at the beginning of each meeting then prayed together with faith and trust in the Lord. Many of the songs contained lyrics from Bible Psalms reinforcing God's mercy and love.

She smiled, warmly reflecting on the close, intimate relationship this small, diverse group of women formed with each other and with the Lord. They all felt their commitment to the prayer group helped them grow closer to God. They all trusted in His promise, *"If you believe, you will receive whatever you ask for in prayer."*

However, through prayer and study, Anne realized some of her prayers were not what God wanted for her. She now learned to end her prayers with the words, "Not my will, but thine be done," and accept the Lord's will in her life.

The doorbell rang interrupting Anne's thoughts. The festivities began. Marie, Nina, and Vanessa's good friend, Sherry, arrived first to help with last minute preparations. Then Uncle Abe and Aunt Marla came with homemade cookies. Leanne and Earl arrived next with fresh Italian bread and the warmth of their friendship.

Anne was glad to spend time with her friends, Mary and Tom who came in from the coast for the party. Both Tom and Mary loved animals. Tom was a veterinarian. When they lived in Austin, they helped Anne and Derek choose their two dogs. Anne hadn't experienced owning a dog before. With Tom and Mary's help, she learned how to care for her dogs. She came to love the warmth and companionship her dogs had to offer. Everyone was glad they were able to make it into town for the party.

Maggie, her close friends from her prayer group, and other close friends all started to arrived with goodies in hand.

The evening quickly flitted by with food, song and laughter. The feeling of friendship and love filled the house with a warm scent of the Christmas season. After the party, Derek and Anne turned the lights low, sat in front of the Christmas tree, and fell asleep in each other's arms.

Anne woke up to the phone ringing early the next morning.

"Anne, this is Mom. I don't want you to get frightened, but I think I just had a slight heart attack. I got a sharp pain that shot through my right arm into my chest. It drained me of all my

energy. Do you think you can take me to the doctor's to get this checked?"

"I'll be there in ten minutes. Should I call an ambulance?"

"No, honey. I'm not in pain now, I just think I should get it checked."

Anne threw on some clothes. She grabbed her coat and rushed to get Marie.

"Mom, you look pale. Let me help you to the car. I don't want you trying to walk by yourself."

Marie chuckled, "Don't worry, I'm not going to drop dead on the way to the car. I'm fine."

"Have you had any symptoms or warning signs of this, Mom?"

"I've had chronic indigestion but the doctor doesn't think it's any big deal. I take Tums and sleep on propped pillows. It bothers me to lie down flat. I've been tired lately, too, but I feel normal other than that."

The doctor was too busy to see Marie, so his Physician's Assistant examined her. "Marie, I think you just have a bad case of indigestion, and stress. I don't think any tests are necessary, but I'll order you an X-ray and an E.K.G." The young man winked at Anne implying he was just placating Marie. He didn't really believe anything at all was wrong.

Anne took Marie to the Lab for the tests ordered. Between the two hour wait and the doctor's gruff attitude both Marie and Anne just wanted to go home and rest.

"You are fine, Mrs. Lanetto. I concur with your doctor. You just have a bad case of indigestion. I'll prescribe some Tagamet for you. It is stronger than the Tums you've been taking. It should get rid of your problem." He looked at his watch and scurried out of the room ignoring Marie's question about what he just prescribed.

"I've had plenty of indigestion in my life. I think he's wrong."

"We'll keep an eye on you, Mom, but if two doctors think the same thing and the test results are all negative, maybe they're right. Let's pick up your prescription and stop for something to eat before I take you home. Maybe that will make you feel a little better."

Anne went down to check on Marie a few days later. She was alarmed at the gaunt, drained look on Marie's face. "Mom, you look terrible. I'm going to call the doctor again."

"Don't bother, they're all full of shit anyway."

Once again the doctor was too busy to see Marie. She was assigned to the same Physician's Assistant.

"Marie, you just have the flu. There really isn't anything I can give you for a virus. Make sure you drink plenty of liquids and get some rest."

Anne, still felt worried and uncomfortable with the way her mother looked. She got Marie settled in and told her to call if she felt any worse.

She called Marie that evening then stopped by the next day. All life was drained from her limbs and her face. She had slipped into a frail exhaustion that rendered her incapable of taking care of herself. Anne called Nina. They both decided to take Marie to the doctor together.

By this time, Marie could not even walk to the car unassisted. She leaned on Anne for support and slumped in the front seat of the car. Anne and Nina insisted on seeing the doctor this time. They refused to leave his office until he was willing to admit her to the hospital for tests.

Their fury with the doctor dissipated when they saw the grave look on his face. "I'm sorry, I had no idea Marie was this bad. I work around the clock most days because many of my patients are elderly. I give the less serious problems to my Physician's Assistant to take care of. He is a good man, and I trust his judgment. You are right, though. Marie needs to go to the hospital right away," he glanced sadly at Marie lying on the table slipping in and out of consciousness.

A few days after Marie was admitted, Anne and Nina met with the Doctor to go over the test results. He lowered his head then looked sadly into their eyes.

"I'm sorry, but your mother has congestive heart failure. It is in a progressed stage. I'm afraid there is little we can do but try to keep her as comfortable as possible. At the most, I believe she has approximately six months to live," his soft voice and moist eyes burned through Anne.

"Can there be any mistake? Are you sure of this? Why didn't the X-ray or E.K.G. she had show any of this?"

"Unfortunately, those tests do not show heart failure. They only show signs of a heart attack. I attribute the occurrence at such an early age as a direct result of cigarettes. I am sorry. Marie is such a good soul. She is one of a kind."

The doctor took time to explain what was going on with Marie's heart and that there was no mistake. "The heart is a dual pump with four chambers, the right and left atrium and the right and left ventricle. It is shaped like a flattened cone a little larger than a fist and is covered by a double-walled sac. It contracts and dilates continuously and rhythmically about one hundred times per day or seventy-two times per minute to transport blood to the lungs and the rest of the body.

"Every tissue and organ requires oxygenated blood for survival. The brain needs an adequate supply or irreversible damage occurs and cerebral tissue disintegrates and dies."

The doctor kept his voice soft and spoke slowly using his hands to illustrate the heart as a large pump.

"Cardiovascular disease is the world's number one killer. Coronary arteries are thread through the heart muscle to provide nourishment. A normal coronary artery transports blood to the myocardium with nothing to impede the flow. A normal coronary artery is only as wide as a straw tapering off at the end. When corrosion builds up, the opening can become so small that blood flow becomes very difficult. From approximately age ten sclerotic material builds up in these vessels and gradually occlude the diameter of the arteries. When the arteries become clogged, oxygenated blood cannot pass the thrombotic area causing myocardial infarction or a heart attack.

"In Marie's case the heart became enlarged and went into failure because it could not handle the excess load of pumping more than usual to carry blood through the heart to the organs.

"In essence, heart failure describes an inability of the heart to keep up its work load. With left-sided heart failure, the heart fails to empty completely with each contraction or has difficulty accepting blood returning from the lungs. The retained blood creates a back pressure causing the lungs to become congested with blood. With right-side failure, there is a back pressure in the blood circulation in the heart causing the liver to become enlarged.

"Marie has seventy-five percent heart failure on both sides of her heart and is already showing signs of liver damage. Medical science attributes a large percentage of the corrosion or atherosclerosis to smoking, poor diet, obesity, lack of exercise and heredity. I believe smoking cut your mother's life by at least five years."

He tried to explain what to expect and urged them to put her in a nursing home where she could have 24 hour a day care. "I am sorry," he ended in a soft voice.

Anne and Nina left the doctor feeling numb and scared for their mother and the days ahead. The profoundness of losing Marie hovered over them like a dark cloud.

"Nina, you call Robert. I'll tell Vanessa, Derek, and the rest of the family. We'll have to meet with Robert here tomorrow and all talk with Mom."

Nina's face exploded with tears. Anne's face remained blank. She felt as though she was walking in a fog. A dark sensation overwhelmed her. She swallowed trying to fight back the fist of anguish gripping her stomach. When she got into her car, she wondered how on earth she could break this to Vanessa.

My God, she gloomily panicked, I don't think I can function without Mom. She's been my rock. She's been my angel in times of distress. She's the only one who really knows me. She always has the right answers when I don't know what to do. Anne's hands trembled as she clung tightly onto the steering wheel. She's always there to pick me up when I fall flat on my face—and God knows I've done that quite a few times in my life. She's always been able to laugh for me when

I couldn't. I can't bear to lose her. How empty life will seem without her.

Anne breathed heavily. She knew a piece of her heart would wither away and die with Marie. She closed her eyes and headed toward the house.

Vanessa was waiting for the news about her Grandmother.

"Hi, honey. I'm afraid the news is not good."

"What do you mean? Grandma is going to be all right, isn't she?"

"I'm afraid not. We're going to lose her, honey. Grandma's heart is in failure. The doctor believes she only has about six months to live."

At first Vanessa glared at her mother in disbelief. Then heavy sobs filled the air echoing the thick pain swelling in Vanessa's heart. Tears flushed over her face while a dizzying rush of panic seeped through her body. Grandma is my best friend, she thought. How can I ever live without her? She ran to her mother. They held onto one another tightly in their grief.

Anne and her family still had gnawing questions about Marie's heart. They all were stunned the doctor didn't discover Marie's condition in time to be able to extend her life. She went to her physician for regular check-ups, but he ignored all the warning signs. They were more convinced than ever that it would have been appropriate to be more assertive and felt Marie's doctor should have been more alert to her condition. They felt years of Marie's vital life had been stolen away from them.

Anne, Nina and Robert had only two days to find a nursing home for Marie. They visited one after the other and were sickened by the condition and odors of most of them. They finally found one they agreed Marie would be comfortable in and went to tell her about it.

Marie bravely soothed her children with words of love. Her strong belief in God clearly demonstrated she was not afraid of what was ahead for her. She displayed the proud dignity she possessed through her life. She continued to reassure her children of their own strengths and encouraged them to stay close to each other and to help one another. She fiercely held onto her courageous sense of humor until the very end.

Fortunately, Nina, Anne, Robert and Vanessa were all able to be with her when she died. After three months of her body slowly giving in to her disease, Marie was ready to let go of this life and journey into the next phase of her being.

She showed her children how to walk through the valley of death with dignity, courage, and hope for a future with the Lord. Her last words were "Open the door, I need to open the door."

Anne believed that was the door to Marie's future with the Lord. She remembered the words she read in Matthew—the very words she clung onto when she and Derek asked the Lord for help with their marriage. It reminded her of the plaque Marie gave them that Christmas.

> *Ask and it will be given to you; seek and you will find; knock and the door will be opened to you. For everyone who asks receives; he who seeks finds; and to him who knocks, the door will be opened...Therefore everyone who hears these words of mine and puts them into practice is like a wise man who built his house on the rock.*

Marie took her final long deep last breath in peace with relief and faith that her next breath would be in a place were the arms of love and serenity awaited her.

Chapter Six

Sacramento 1989-92

Shit, he thought. I've got to get my act together. I can't go on like this. He shook his thick dark hair wiping the sweat from his forehead. He hacked to clear his lungs then headed to his mother's.

"Hi, Mom," his voice quivered when Marsha opened the door.

"Rick, my God, what have you been up to? You look sick!" Marsha said. Her son's frail look startled her. Even though he tried to smile reassuringly, his gaunt cheeks and ashen face frightened her.

"Well, I haven't been doing too good on my own, Mom. In fact, you could say I'm homeless." A moment of awkward silence ripped into Marsha's flesh. Rick shuffled his feet nervously and clenched his hand around the post on the porch.

"Do you think I could come home for awhile?" he quietly asked leaning against the post with his head down.

"Come on in, honey," Marsha said with a frustrated sigh. "Let's get you something to eat."

Rick put one hand up to his mouth and the other against his chest and coughed.

"You need to get some cough medicine to get rid of that. It sounds pretty bad," Marsha tenderly commented.

He raked his shaking fingers through a strand of his thick hair pushing it back, "Yeah, I know. I've been meaning to. I just haven't had a chance."

Rick ate a sandwich and some soup then headed for his room. Fatigue weighed down his leg muscles, but he threw Marsha a deep smile that crinkled the corners of his eyes so she wouldn't suspect just how bad he felt.

"I was on my way to work. You get some rest. We'll talk later."

"Okay, Mom. Thanks," he said flashing a grin of tenderness then blew her a kiss. He laid down resting the back of his arm on his forehead. The comfort of his old bed engulfed him into a black cloud of sleep.

Over the next few weeks Rick tried to change. Marsha, pleased with Rick's decision to turn over a new leaf, did everything she could to encourage his efforts. She made his favorite meals; they went to some baseball games together just like old times and put aside special times for the two of them to renew their friendship and enjoy each other's company.

Marsha sat at the kitchen table after dinner trying to complete her math homework for a class she was taking. Rick noticed her look of frustration and went over to help. He recognized her silent plea for help by the way her left eyebrow tilted up and the corner of her mouth drew into a tight line as a frown played on her lips.

"Let me take a look at this for you, Mom," he offered rubbing the top of her shoulders.

Marsha sighed in relief and smiled. She wished her Math

ability was as good as Rick's. He had a way of pointing out how to tackle problems in a simple and clear way. When he explained the problems, the animation on his face brought back sweet memories of his childhood, his zest for life, and his dry sense of humor.

His infinite patience with her and determination to help her through her homework gave Marsha a warm feeling of hope for her son. She was glad they had a chance to go to some games together again. She fondly thought of his soccer games and how proud she was of him when he played.

"Thanks, honey. I could have never finished this without your help."

"Yes you could have. It just would have taken a little longer," Rick said warmly encouraging his mother.

"At any rate, when I get back from class tonight, I'll bake your favorite cookies. How's that sound?"

"Ill never turn down your homemade cookies," he said rubbing his hands together, throwing a smiling wink to Marsha.

"I better get going, or I'll be late."

"Okay. I'll see you tonight," he said running to answer the phone as Marsha closed the door.

"Hello."

"Hey, Rick, this is Johnny. How's it goin?"

"It's going okay. How about with you?"

"Not bad. Pretty good in fact. I got some good dope. You want to party?"

"I don't know, John. I've been trying to stay away from the stuff."

"Hey, my man, this is some fine stuff and everyone's going to be here. Come on, just one night. Everyone's been asking about you."

"Well...okay. I'll come by in about an hour, but I can't stay too long."

"All right! See ya then."

Rick hung up. He went in to change clothes feeling a tinge of excitement mixed with doubt about the party. It's only one night, he thought. I can handle it. He threw a pack of cough drops in his shirt pocket and headed to Johnny's.

Linda opened the door. She threw her arm around Rick's neck bringing him into the house. "Hey look who's here!" she exclaimed staggering.

"Rick! Perfect timing. Come on over here and have a hit. This is great stuff," Johnny slurred excitedly.

Rick strode into the smoky room filled with friends, booze and drugs.

"Yeah, just like old times," he softly said under his breath reaching for the beer Linda handed him. The muscles in his thin neck strained as he took a hit of meth. He involuntarily gagged, and a smile tugged at the corners of his mouth when he felt the meth rush into his lungs. He held in the smoke as deep and as long as possible. He felt it surge through his body. The wild tingle he had come to love filled his limbs with voluptuous ecstasy.

"This is great," he said pulling Linda closer for a kiss. "Why have I stayed away so long? I must have been out of my mind," he laughed nuzzling the back of Linda's neck playfully. She giggled smiling into his darkly handsome features. The quick flash of fire in his eyes excited her. She threw him a playful grin sliding her fingers down his back, hoping she would find him in her arms after the party.

With each hit, Marsha's homemade cookies and his promise of sobriety drifted further from his mind. His face felt tight and warm from laughter, but his chest hurt from the smoke. The music and voices of his friends swirled in his head when he tried to focus on Linda's face.

"Come on, Rick, let's go upstairs," Linda softly whispered in his ear flashing a teasing look. She had waited all night and wanted him now. She tauntingly rubbed the front of his pants hoping she could find some crack she could slip out of his pocket before they crashed. It was 2:30 A.M. The party was dying. Only a few friends lingered either passed out on the floor or in a chair. His mouth bent gently to take hers while she coaxed him with the caress of her firm tender hands. A faint smile bordered his lips when Linda led him down the hall into the bedroom. He gently took her face into his broad hands and began kissing every part of the soft flesh on her ivory tinted face. Disappointed he had no dope stashed in his pants, she decided to enjoy the sensations he so skillfully brought out in her. She pushed her body firmly against his. Her head fell back to the warmth of his wet lips pressing on her skin. Wild free passion exploded. She arched against him deeply responding to his soft pulsing lips. Waves of exhilaration slammed through them in unison as their bodies met with passionate force. The wide spread of his legs pressed against her thighs passionately pounded into her flesh.

A low guttural moan escaped from the back of her throat as she slid her hands through his hair moving down to his shoulders and across his lean, muscular back. She clutched onto him with her fingernails digging slightly into his skin. The roughness of the slight growth on his face scaled her cheeks intensifying her pleasure. They crushed each other with each bolting movement driving away all sense of time until ecstatic exhaustion crept in, and they passed out in each other's arms.

Marsha sat at the kitchen table staring at the clock. It was 3:00 A.M., and Rick was still not home. She took a bite out of a cookie she made him earlier. Shimmering tears in her eyes slowly released drops on her cheeks. Devasted by the sudden awareness that tonight's behavior showed Rick slipping back into his old habits, wild impatience and worry overcame Marsha.

Trying to calm her raw nerves and terror, she took a pill to help her sleep. With a sickening rush of pain, his empty promises rattled in her mind. She fiercely wanted to believe he had changed for good, but her sixth sense issued an acute warning that tonight would be the beginning of Rick's old pattern emerging. Her intangible, gut wrenching feeling flashed warning signals setting her teeth on edge. She dizzily struggled for composure. Mild irritation settled into sad rage as the dark of night slowly seeped into daylight.

Over the next few months Marsha grew increasingly worried over Rick's erratic behavior and his irritating tendency to come home late or not at all. She hoped he would outgrow his rejection to settle down, and that he would overcome his impulsive tendency to do whatever pleased him without looking ahead to the consequences of his behavior, or how it effected other people in his life.

As she dressed for work, she smiled and thought of his compelling smile, springy black hair, mischievous dark eyes, and his gentle voice. Then she tightened her lips with annoyance. She gloomily shook her head with thoughts of his flaring temper, restless anxiety, and passive refusal to change. Even Jessica was unable to convince him to slow down and think about a stable future.

Marsha rounded her lips to put the last touch of lipstick on and caught Rick's reflection in the mirror behind her. A twinkling grin flashed his white teeth highlighting his bronze features and firm jaw. Marsha's gaze searched her son's eyes. Through his smile she sensed a hollow, intense shadow of restlessness in the dark thick lashed windows to his soul. He coughed, trying to quiet the harsh rattling sound in his chest.

"Don't look so serious, Mom. You need to relax a little," he teased.

"How can I relax with the hours you keep? It has to stop, Rick. I have to get to work, but I want to talk to you tonight. Will you pick me up some ground meat for dinner at the corner market and make sure you're home by 5:30 for dinner?"

"Okay, Mom, I'll be here." He kissed the top of her head and left the room as suddenly as he came in.

Marsha closed her eyes, took a deep breath, and headed for work trying to calm her sickened heart of its foreboding flutters.

Rick walked into his room. He threw a brush through his hair then tucked his shirt in his jeans. Grabbing his keys he walked down to the corner grocery store to buy the ground meat for dinner. He rubbed his temples as he walked trying to soothe the ache in his head. Mom's right, he thought. I do need to slow down a little.

He looked up at the stark blue sky devoid of any clouds. The sun blazing down on the back of his shoulders felt good but did not take away the clammy chill he felt. I think I'll get some rest after I get the groceries then I'll call Sis. It's time I got over to see my little nephew. He's quite a guy, he smiled thinking of the loose curls of sandy blonde hair and the gentle blue eyes on his nephew's delicate heart-shaped face.

By the time he got to the store, Rick was tired and out of breath. He intended to pick up groceries for the week but decided to just get a few things and get home. He strolled down the isle and picked up a bag of chips and cookies then headed for the meat department.

He gasped raggedly trying to control his coughing. I think I'll pick up some cough medicine too. I feel like shit, he thought as he examined the different labels on the medicine. I was cold just a while ago, now I feel like I'm burning up. I need to get home and lay down for awhile. He put a bottle in his basket and walked slowly to the check out stand.

"That will be $15.35," the checkout girl stated stunned at the glazed, pale-ash look on Rick's face and the sweat on his brow. Rick fumbled for the money and stepped shakily forward to get his bag. He wandered toward the door, but the room spun and faded into a black hole.

"Somebody call an ambulance!" a woman huffed as she ran to the store manager. "A boy has collapsed by the front entrance. I noticed him waver as he walked toward the door. Then he dropped his bag and his knees folded forward. He's lying face down. I can't tell if he is still breathing," she spit in fast breathy words.

The manager quickly ran toward Rick. He shook his shoulder and called out to him but got no response. "Everybody stay calm, I'll call an ambulance," he blurted jolting toward the phone.

"We need an ambulance right away. One of our patrons has collapsed. He's lying face down on the floor. He's not moving, but he still seems to be breathing. No, I can't tell if he needs C.P.R. No, I don't know how to administer it. I'll see if anyone else does, but you'd better hurry."

The shaken manager hung up and called out, "Does anyone know C.P.R.?" His eyes darted through the scared faces. He mumbled to himself with agitation, "Damn, that ambulance better hurry. Shit. Why did this have to happen on my shift?"

The hospital attendant found Marsha's phone number. He called her as soon as Rick was wheeled into the Emergency Room. Marsha's chin tensed, and her voice rose passionately as she tried to pry more information out of the caller.

"What do you mean he's unconscious?" she said with an explosion of terror clutching onto the phone. "I'll be right there," she added in a weak course stammer finding her throat closed into a tight knot. Sharp tiny needles pinched at Marsha's face while she drove to the hospital. She quickly parked. Then she grabbed her bag from the car and ran through the Emergency door to the front desk.

"I'm Richard Tess's mother. He was brought in here a few minutes ago. I'd like to see him please," she blurted.

"We need you to fill in some papers first, Mrs. Tess," the young blonde receptionist stated plainly.

Marsha snatched the papers moving slightly forward looking directly into the clerk's eyes. "My son is here—you take me to him, or I'll find him myself. I'll fill in your damn paperwork AFTER I see him," she breathed in a low forceful voice.

Marsha stared steadily as the girl's pink cheeks reddened and her rose colored, overly made-up lips tightened. She fluttered her heavily darkened lashes and pointed the way for Marsha to find Rick. Marsha abruptly turned slightly holding her breath as she approached his room.

She gawked in amazement and stood in rigid silence wincing at the contraptions hooked up to her son. She felt her aimless surge of energy drain. She stared at Rick's pale blue lips quivering and his limbs lying lifeless by his side. The doctor gently took Marsha to the side, explaining Rick's lungs collapsed due to pneumonia probably agitated by the drugs he had been taking.

"I'm sorry, Mrs. Tess, but Rick's stability is tenuous at this time. I'm not sure he will pull through. We will keep him as comfortable as possible, though, and assist his breathing with a respirator."

Indignant revulsion flushed Marsha with an all consuming pain and grief. Big heaving breaths of sobs shook her shoulders. She stood there finding her life melting into a nightmare. When her trembling died away, she slowly approached her son stroking his hand. She prayed God would rescue them, quietly refusing to believe the reality of her shattered hopes and dreams for her child.

A harsh blow of pain stabbed at her heart as her tear-stained eyes witnessed each precious minute chiseling away the remaining vitality in her son's life. She prayed he could hold onto any shred of his remaining strength.

"Come on, sweetheart, you can get through this. I know you can," she whispered. She remembered the fierce determination to live he had as a newborn. She searched his face for a long uncomfortable moment nestling her warm cheek against the back of his hand and hummed softly. Swallowing the large lump in her throat, her memory vividly pictured their shared hopes, dreams, disappointments, friendship, trust, and love as her voice strained melodiously in a soft quiet hum to her son.

AUSTIN 1991-92

A ray of sunlight edged through a sliver in the window blinds shimmering gracefully over the carpet. Finding its way across the room, it splashed softly touching Anne's delicate pink cheek. Anne stretched one arm out then the other enjoying the warmth of her bed. She let out a low sigh. Pushing off the covers, she dangled her feet over the side of the bed. Anne slowly shuffled to the blind to open it. She let the sunshine fully hit her face. The bright warmth permeated through her body bringing it to life.

She went in to make her morning cup of tea. She brought it to the back porch along with her two dogs, her cordless phone, and her Bible. She watched the wildlife, read, and enjoyed a little more of the sun. Golden threads of light rested on Casey's soft fur. She wagged her tail and gently nudged Anne to pet the top of her head while Kaley dashed after a butterfly flitting across the backyard.

Anne closed her eyes resting her head on the back of the glider while stroking Casey's warm fur. It had been three months since she lost Marie. The loneliness and depression was starting to take hold in spite of the support and encouragement from her friends and family. She felt a sense of peace for her mother but missed the sound of her voice and the comfort of her friendship. The thought of never touching her hand or sharing warm intimate feelings with Marie made her shudder.

She missed Marie's warm laughter. She missed her friendship. She missed hearing the sound of her voice.

Anne contacted her father to let him know Marie was dying. She had only heard his voice a few times since he left thirty years ago. Nina and Robert were unhappy with her decision to contact him. They wanted nothing to do with him. Anne, however, felt drawn to initiate some level of contact.

Although frightened at the prospect of rejection, she gathered the nerve to call him again when Marie died. She asked if he was interested in any kind of a relationship with her. After all, Anne thought, in the Lord's Prayer it says, "And forgive us our sins as we forgive those who sin against us."

Anne talked with Marie before she died about reconciling with her father. Marie encouraged her and reminded Anne that the word "forgiveness" is strewn throughout God's teachings.

> *Let all bitterness and wrath and anger and clamor and slander be put away from you, with all malice, and be kind to one another, tenderhearted, forgiving one another, as God in Christ forgave you.*

Anne felt she must put aside feelings of bitterness against her father. She believed it was not for her to judge his actions but for the Lord only to judge. She felt what her father did to her mother and her family was not right and was not what God would have wanted him to do, but she also believed that issue would have to be placed in God's hands. She no longer wanted bitterness and hate to rule her mind and her spirit. She prayed for God's help to truly forgive and to protect her from being hurt again. Rocco seemed uneasy about starting a relationship, but with time, they got reacquainted through occasional letters and phone calls.

Anne looked out in the yard again smiling at her two dogs. They loved prancing about in the fresh air. Anne inhaled then drew her attention to her recent peculiar, nagging concerns for her son. She didn't understand why, but couldn't shake a pressing uncomfortable feeling that her son needed her. She was used to thinking about him but this was different. It was an edgy feeling of a brewing storm. It felt like low growling clouds and a dark sullen sky was enclosing around her.

Anne experienced gut feelings like her mother did. She had an uncanny way of sensing a problem before any physical sign of the problem itself manifested, like a premature valve turning on to distinguish a fire merely smoldering or the low murmur of a volcano before it erupts. The hair on her arms would stand on end. She would feel a jittery sense of forewarning in the pit of her stomach. Through the years Anne learned to recognize these feelings and give them credence rather than brushing them off.

She recently began to study about the gifts of the Holy Spirit. She prayed His light and love would guide her to her son. She read literature and Scripture describing the Holy Spirit as an equal part of the Trinity. She believed the Father, Son, and Holy Spirit are one and all are equal in every way. The Father created Adam and Eve and were with them at the beginning of mankind. The Son came thousands of years ago to be with mankind and to save us. The Holy Spirit is with us now, guiding us, giving us courage and strength, providing us with His gifts to enable us to walk in His light on earth and to enter our home in his heavenly kingdom. She believed the Holy Spirit is the Comforter and Helper who strengthens and empowers.

Anne picked up her Bible and turned to the section in Corinthians. It describes spiritual gifts and explains that there are different kinds of gifts such as Wisdom, Knowledge, and Faith, but the same Spirit. There are different kinds of service, but the same Lord. There are different kinds of working, but the same God works all of them in all men.

Anne began to understand that we each have been given gifts, and that it is our responsibility to tap into our gifts and use them for the good of the Lord. She also recognized that we are not given any of these gifts because we are deserving or more important that someone else. We are given these gifts so that God may use us as vehicles to spread His word through mankind and to manifest His presence in the world.

Anne breathed in trying to sift through and untangle the love and guilt welling inside her filling her chest with a dull pain. In the past, she learned to suppress any emotion of love when she thought of her son. She believed she had no right to feel anything but shame. Then she discovered an organization that provided support to her, and other parents, children, and siblings separated by the adoption process. They talked about their desire to reunite with support and encouragement.

Anne discovered this organization and similar organizations challenge the chronic injustice of the singular use of the "closed" adoption system which prohibits a birth mother and her child future contact after final adoption papers are signed. Anne realized she was forced to use the "closed" adoption process when she relinquished her son because no other type of adoption was available. "Closed" adoption severed the link between Anne and her son forever by permanently prohibiting contact between them with sealed records. Anne's documents, as all other "closed" adoption documents, remain sealed and restricted by law from view or duplication by the public.

Anne discovered through the group that she had not only a right to feel for her son, but it was a natural instinct she no longer needed to suppress. She began reading books in the library about adoption and attended monthly meetings to learn how to begin a search for her son. She wondered how differently things might have been had "open" adoption been legal at the time of her son's birth. She wondered at what level of contact, if any, she and the adoptive parents would have been comfortable with, and how different things might be now.

Anne found it hard to believe that still, twenty years later, only a glimmer of recognition for reform was slowly creeping into our system. Since she belonged to the search group she realized not nearly enough progress had been made to overturn the laws etched in stone. They ruthlessly hold the fates of millions of people in its locked files. Anne, like many others, felt the antiquated laws etched in granite passively ignore wounds that will never heal until reform and counseling take place.

The phone rang interrupting Anne thoughts. "Hi, honey. I just called to say good morning."

"Hi, Derek. I'm sitting on the back porch enjoying the sun with the dogs."

"That's good, Anne. I was a little worried about you. You've been tossing and turning all week. Is there anything you need to talk about?"

"No, I just am concerned over my uneasy feelings about my son. I've written the adoption agency three times and placed a waiver of confidentiality in my file to permit the agency to give my son information on me if he inquires, but I still feel uneasy. I had such high hopes that he would have also placed a waiver of confidentiality in his file. Then we could have been reunited. I wonder why he hasn't. Do you think he doesn't want to have anything to do with me?"

"I think that's possible, Anne, but you need to think more positive. He is only twenty years old. Maybe he'll want to find you when he's a little older."

"I don't want to wait till he's older, Derek. I've already lost twenty years of his life. I don't want to wait another day. I sometimes feel like my skin is crawling. I do thank God for all we have and especially that Vanessa's back on the right track. But I can't stop focusing on my son.

"I'm so grateful you and Vanessa not only accepted the news about my situation with my son but have supported me 100 percent. You'll never know how much that means to me.

I never thought I would find the courage to tell you about it let alone to admit to Vanessa I lied about having a baby that died.

"Even though I know she's still struggling with her own issues and continually battling setbacks, she's still been supportive of my search. I know she has a long way to go, but I hope with her continual efforts to overcome her problems, she will find peace and settle into a more positive way of life. You know, Derek, going through this with Vanessa makes me feel like I'm constantly walking on an unsteady tightrope. My heart aches with helpless recognition that relapse is always just a breath away. I've become convinced intervention and intense counseling are imperative to work through the destructive tendencies cocaine and other drugs draw you into. They can devour you and rob you of everything if you give in to the evil pleasure they seduce you with. I've been so proud of her though. She's been trying real hard to stay off the drugs, and has given me understanding and support without judgment. She can be one fine young lady, can't she?"

"Yes she can, Anne. We both love you very much, but you're right. She does have a long way to go. We have to continually pray for her and other young people who have fallen prey to this terrible affliction. It not only effects them—it impacts their entire family. Listen, honey, I want you to put on something special tonight. I'm going to take you out for dinner. I'm getting a little worried about you. You need to take your mind off everything for a while."

"Okay, I promise I'll have a nice big smile for you when you come home."

"That's my girl. I'll see you around 5:30."

Anne hung up the phone. She decided to walk a couple of miles with the dogs to take her mind off something she could not change for the time being. Walking always helped Anne clear her mind and relax.

The next five months brought Anne no closer to finding her son. She got up and kissed Derek good morning. She then sipped her cup of tea and read the Saturday paper. After she noticed the mailman, she opened the door as usual letting her two dogs run and play in the yard. She walked down to the mailbox at the end of the driveway to see if there was yet any word from the agency.

Anne's eyes widened when she pulled a letter from the box and read the return address of the social service agency she was trying to get the information from. She called her dogs and sprang into the house. At last, she thought ripping open the envelope as she leapt to the house to show Derek.

"Derek!" Anne screamed waving the letter to her husband. "It's here, I finally got the letter from the agency! I've written three times in the past five months and called them four times. I guess my persistence has finally paid off." Anne held the letter scanning its words then her wide smile quickly melted into a puzzled frown.

"What's wrong, Anne?"

"I don't believe it! I've been contacting the wrong adoption agency all this time, and they didn't have the decency to tell me until now. In my last letter I sent them a $50 check. I hoped they would hire someone overtime to find my files since they said they were so overwhelmed with work. They returned my check, and said they are not even the right agency! Why did they waste five months of precious time?" Tears welled in her eyes as she stammered, "I don't understand how they could do this? Why did they keep stalling and making pathetic excuses that their work overload rendered them unable to research my file for the non-identifying information I was seeking?

"Gari-Sue, the leader of our adoption group, informed me I have a right to seek non-identifying information from the adoption agency concerning the adopting parents." Anne's voice, racing faster and getting louder as she rambled on to Derek, suddenly crumbled.

He went to her and put his arms around her letting her cry. "Anne, I'm sorry, honey," he soothed her. "Let me take a look at that letter."

Derek read the letter taking Anne's face in his hands and

looked deep into her eyes. "At least they gave you the name of the right agency, Anne. Just look at this as a set back. You can have a letter off to this agency tomorrow."

Anne pulled back drying her eyes. "You're right. I'm going to type a letter right now. I'll have you check over it before I mail it, okay?"

Anne went into the office and frantically began typing. All right, she thought to herself, let me review my notes on non-identifying information. It is important to get this right because it might give me some clues to help me locate my son.

She began reading slowly...It is any information other than that which would lend to identifying a member of the biological or adoptive family, but sometimes clues can be found in a search from the information. She read the literature and reviewed the types of questions she could ask such as what was the occupation of the adoptive parents, how long had they been married, are there any other children in the family, what reasons did the parents give for wanting to adopt, what information was given at follow up visits to the child, etc.

Adoptees can ask things like what were my birth parents' first names, what was the reason for relinquishment, were my birth parents married to each other, what medical information is listed, what was the age of my birth parents, do I have siblings, what state were they from, etc.

Anne's fingers typed speedily. She was determined to have her letter ready for the mail the first thing in the morning. She hoped the answer to her questions would alleviate some of the restlessness she felt. She stayed up until two in the morning writing and rewriting the letter making sure her questions were just right. When she finally went to bed, frustration and a growing concern for her son made another sleepless night fade into weeks.

She spent the next few weeks on pins and needles with anticipation. Once again she approached the mailbox hoping today would be the day she would receive their response, and it was.

This time Anne held the letter in her hands without opening it. She plodded into the house and stared at the envelope. She picked up the phone to call her friend Maggie. "Hi Mag, it's me."

"Hi, Anne, how are you?"

"I'm all right. I just received the letter from the adoption agency in the mail. Do you want to hear what it says?"

"Yes! Hurry up and open it Anne. Read it to me."

We received your Waiver of Confidentiality form and filed it in your case. This letter is in response to your request for information about the adoptive parents to your son.

Your son was placed with a couple in their late 20s. They had been married around ten years and had a stable marriage. The father was of average build with brown eyes, black hair, and light olive skin. He was of Irish, German, and French descent. He grew up back East and had one brother. He was Catholic. The mother was short with medium build. She had blue eyes, brown hair, and fair skin. She was of French, German, Irish, and English descent. She grew up back East and had seven siblings. She was Presbyterian.

Although he had not completed high school, the father had a good job in sales as an assistant to the vice president. He regretted his lack of education and had taken some classes. He was described as responsible and aggressive, having a strong personality. The mother was a high school graduate who had worked as a secretary.

The couple had a little girl who was in elementary school. She had brown eyes and hair and looked like her father. She was described as a curious and imaginative child. She did well at school. The couple wanted more children and attempted two more pregnancies which were not successful due to a medical problem.

This couple enjoyed family life. Their activities

included bowling, miniature golf, movies, tennis, and going to the beach. The mother was involved in PTA and Brownies, and she liked to sew, crochet, and paint. They lived in a city and were buying their home. They had a cat.

The father was pleased with the Italian heritage of your son as he had business dealings with an Italian company. In fact, he said he would like to live there for a year or two. During the agency's supervision period, your son did well. The little girl wanted to mother him and was proud of him. He was christened.

I hope this information is helpful to you. This is really all that we can disclose to you in view of the confidentiality of adoption records.

Anne's voice faded.

"Anne, are you all right?"

"I'm okay, Mag, I just need time to digest all of this. They told me so much yet so little."

"Listen, Anne, why don't you take some time to read over the letter some more, and call me later when you're up to it."

"That sounds good, Maggie. Thanks."

Anne read and reread the letter until her eyes could not focus any longer. She showed Derek when he came home then told him she made plans with Nina to walk in the park after dinner.

She went into her office to focus on the letter. She closely examined every word for any fragment of a clue to help her locate her son. Although it answered so many questions, it also stirred even more questions in her mind. She called Gari-Sue, and she advised Anne to write a follow-up letter with her additional questions.

Nina hurriedly cleaned up after dinner so she could get to Anne's early. After seven years of raising her son alone, Nina found a down-to-earth, quiet, sensitive man to settle down with. Not only were they compatible and happy with one another, but he displayed a genuine interest in Samuel. Nina kissed her two gentlemen good-bye and headed for Anne's anxious to read the letter. When Anne answered the door, Nina was surprised she was not more enthusiastic about the letter. She read the letter but remained uncomfortable with the look on Anne's face.

"I won't be too long, Derek," Anne said sweeping a kiss over his lips and grabbing her keys. She and Nina avoided the topic of the letter as they drove to the park. Nina parked, and they immediately set off walking briskly around the park.

"Anne, you don't seem satisfied with the letter," Nina carefully stated during their walk.

"I'm glad I got the letter, Nina, but it didn't quench my restlessness at all. I still feel like there is something going on with my son. They gave me very little to go on to try to find him on my own. I called Gari-Sue at the search organization I belong to. She advised me to write again."

"If you're not satisfied with the letter, then you should write again."

"I wish I could remember more, but my mind is blank. I couldn't even remember the right social service agency I used. I seem to have blocked that entire time period out of my mind. I don't know what to do to remember more. I can't even remember the name of the hospital I delivered the baby or the street I lived on. How could I totally erase all of that information out of my mind?"

"It was a very painful time for you, Anne. I think it is a defense mechanism on your part. Maybe if you relax a little things will start to come to you."

"I've tried everything to retrieve information from my mind, Nina, but nothing has worked so far. I think all I can do at this point is write another letter. Maybe that will help."

During the next month Anne attended a meeting to ask for help devising another letter to the agency and to air her frustrations. Gari-Sue helped Anne write a new letter which she sent off the following day.

Another three weeks of anticipation kept Anne on edge. Her casual walk to the mailbox slithered into a daily intense, rapid gait. On the way to the mailbox, Anne tried to relax her clenched jaw and the contracted muscles in her neck. She felt an April wisp of a warm breeze splash through her waves, teasing tiny strands of hair through its fingers and onto Anne's cheek. Anne thrived on the sensual beauty April brought out in Austin. It held an uncanny ability to soothe her stress and anticipation.

Anne approached the bottom of the driveway. She stepped toward the mailbox and reached in with deliberation slowly pulling out the long awaited letter. Bringing the letter to her chest, she closed her eyes with relief and exhilaration. By the time she reached the front door, Anne already had begun to carefully study the reply to her second inquiry.

> *Our letter to you contained very general, non-specific information because we have to protect the confidentiality of the adoptive family, as we do the birth parents. The record states that the adopting father was Catholic and the mother was Presbyterian. It did not state which religion they planned to rear the child in, although it did indicate that he was christened. The adoptive parents had not lived in Italy although the father had been there on business. He wanted to go live there for a while, but the mother was happy here. Their house was not described in the case record.*
>
> *The mother was healthy. She had lost two pregnancies, but had no other medical problems. Your son was placed with his adoptive parents when he was three months old. The parents met with his neurologist who felt he was neurologically normal and the only risk would be in the area of intellectual functioning. At six months of age, the child had another neurological examination. The neurologist said he was fine and there was no need for him to return unless he showed some sign of developmental lag.*
>
> *In April, 1972, he was described as a handsome,*

plump child with large dark eyes and wavy hair. He had an outgoing personality and the parents were well-satisfied with his development. Their parenting style included giving him a lot of freedom and stimulation. At that time, our agency surpervised adoptive placements for around a year. The last time we had contact with the family, the child was normal and healthy.

In May 1981, we did receive a call from the adoptive mother. She was going to take her son back to the neurologist because he was having some muscle spasms and tics. After that, we did not hear anything further from them. Unless your son completes and submits a Waiver form, we cannot give you any more specific information. We hope this is helpful to you.

Once again Anne was left with an empty, gnawing, unsatisfied feeling she couldn't shake. She felt concerned the adoptive mother called when her son was ten to mention muscle spasms and tics. Why would they wait so many years then call about a problem unless it was significant? She had to find out more. She sent another letter to the agency questioning her son's health. She urged them to give her all the medical information they had on file. In the meantime, she began calling hospitals in the San Francisco area to find out where she delivered her son.

After unsuccessfully questioning fourteen hospitals, she called her father in California to see if he could find the hospital or any information for her. After Marie's death, her relationship with her father continued. She knew nothing could change the lost years or justify the mistakes made, but they continued to mend their broken relationship.

"Hi, Dad, this is Anne."

"Hello, Anne. How are you?"

"Well the truth of the matter is I've been searching for my son I gave away twenty years ago in California. I have been running into one stumbling block after the other hitting my head repeatedly against the system. I seem to be getting nowhere. I understand you've kept contact with my cousin, Cecelia, I briefly stayed with in San Francisco when I was pregnant. I was hoping you might be able to find out from her what hospital I gave birth to my son. I thought that information might be helpful to me."

"I'll call her and find out what I can. I can't make any promises, but my son, Jerry, works in a hospital here in California. I don't know if he can, but I'll see if he might be able to find out something."

"That would be wonderful. Please tell him I would appreciate any information at all." Anne recently met her half-brother, Jerry . Nina and Robert still wanted nothing to do with their father, but they were receptive to a relationship with Jerry. They all met and felt good about the meeting.

Rocco also had a daughter in his second marriage, but she didn't seem interested in pursuing a relationship with Anne and her family. Although Anne felt a little disappointed about that, she was glad their meeting with Jerry was so successful and was happy she got to know him. She hung up praying Jerry might be able to help her and shook her head wondering why she couldn't remember.

By the time she received the answer to her third letter, it was June. Her fingers fumbled, yanking at the letter to read it contents.

I am sorry for the delay in answering your letter. After your son was born, brain damage was suspected. A neurologist gave him an examination at age three weeks. He said the exam was "not very remarkable." The child had tremors of his chin but there appeared to be "no gross damage to the nervous system." Nevertheless, the doctor said the "outlook for intellectual development was guarded," and it was "not possible to make any assessment of future intellectual development at this time." He said intellectual damage might not show up until 2-3 years of age, or even not until the child entered school. He remarked his apparent soundness of condition was astounding in view of the seriousness of the problem at birth.

Around age three months, your son was examined again by the neurologist. He said the child "seemed more normal than ever." He discussed the child's condition with the adoptive parents, and asked them to bring the child back in at age six months. At the six month examination, no problems were noted, and the parents were told that there was no need for him to return unless he showed some sign of developmental lag. The adoption was finalized and our case was closed. Then, in 1981 we received a call from the adoptive mother. She said her son was having muscle spasms and tics, and she had made and appointment with a neurologist. The doctors's office wanted from us the name the child had when he was in foster care so they could pull his old chart. The supervisor then called the adoptive mother. The adoptive mother joked, "You can't have him back!" Unfortunately, we have had no follow-up calls from the adoptive mother to give us any updated medical information. When a case is closed, we no longer contact the family. If the client contacts us, we do respond.

Our record at the time you relinquished, you said if you had the means, you would most assuredly keep your child. You realized the best plan for the child would be to give it a home by adoption. It appears you have agonized over this for years and continue to grieve. As we do not know how your son is, we can give you no updated information. ***Many parents who relinquish a child find counseling helpful. You might consider this.***

You could contact a local adoption agency for information on search, support groups, and consultants, and contact the International Soundex Reunion Registry. The ISRR keeps a computer listing, or registry, and will cross-reference and match adoptees and birth parents whenever information is received. We hope this information is helpful to you.

"Many parents who relinquish a child find counseling helpful. You might consider this," she read out loud in an unpleasant flat tone then again in a raised voice of disbelief.

How dare they, she raged. I'm not the one who needs counseling. They do! Once again she found herself at the mercy of the apathetic system and its worker bees. They found her persistence and concern vaguely irritating, somewhat like a sticky bug that needed to be flicked away and squashed.

They displayed about as much feeling as one would have when a bug splatters on your windshield—slightly cringing at the inconvenience and nuisance of washing the bug off rather than feeling any concern for its exploded body. She stomped out of the house and ran until she had no energy left. Her mind drifted to the story in Luke.

One of the Pharisees invited Jesus to dinner with him. A woman who lived a sinful life in that town learned Jesus was eating there.

She brought an alabaster jar of perfume, stood behind him at his feet weeping and wet his feet with her tears. Then she wiped them with her hair, kissed them and poured perfume on them. When the Pharisee saw this, he said to himself, If this man were a prophet, he would know who is touching him and what kind of woman she is—that she is a sinner.

Jesus said to him, "Two men owed money to a certain moneylender. One owed him five hundred denarii, and the other fifty. Neither of them had the money to pay him back, so he canceled the debts of both. Now which of them will love him more?

Simon replied, I suppose the one who had the bigger debt canceled.

You have judged correctly, Jesus said.

He turned toward the woman and said to Simon, "Do you see this woman? I came into your house. You did not give me any water for my feet, but she wet my feet with her tears and wiped them with her hair. You did not give me a kiss, but this woman, from the time I entered, has not stopped kissing my feet. You did not put oil on my head, but she has poured perfume on my feet. Therefore, I tell you, her many sins have been forgiven—for she loved much.

Anne breathed heavily and whispered, "Please forgive me. Help me to forgive myself. I believe my son was better off being raised by someone stable with the kind of love I was not able to give him at the time. But, Lord, there's a part of me that feels sickened and makes my heart burn with shame, guilt, and contempt for myself.

"All the rationalization in the world doesn't ease the pain. How can I so strongly believe what I did what was best for my son and still feel locked in such utter feelings of remorse? Lord, I, too, have so much for you to forgive. I know I am not worthy, but please forgive me."

Tears of defeat and disgust burned down her cheeks. Her mind raced. Her fears escalated gripping her chest like an iron fist. She recited, "The Lord is with you when you are with him. If you seek him, he will be found by you."

She massaged her temples then tilted her head to the sky and moaned, "Where are you, Lord? Please help me. I don't have enough information to find him on my own. I need you." She abruptly stopped then straightened her shoulders.

She let her mind wonder to the image of Jesus walking in a garden with joy over his creation. Then he took on the flesh of man. She imagined Him experiencing the simple pleasures of tasting fresh juice from a fruit tree, looking at the beauty of a sunset, and feeling the warmth of a light rain trickling down his face. She then envisioned Him allowing himself to experience the agony and defeat of pain and of suffering.

Anne visualized a rainbow of light between her and a gentle, loving God wading in a river with his bare feet. She imagined his shirt sleeves rolled up. He tossed his head back letting the breeze catch his hair. She felt his eyes crinkle touching her in a warm smile. At that moment, she felt his forgiveness. She resolved she must let nothing stop her from finding her son.

Chapter Seven

SACRAMENTO 1992

Marsha hovered over Rick. Her eyes remained fixed in a trance like stare at the tubes running through his nose, mouth, and stiff, bloated arms. She softly stroked his limp hands. She tried to focus through the tears pasted in her eyes. Her head sagged as she forced her eyes away from the tubes and rested them on her son's expressionless face.

She felt Rick's presence last night. Today the room felt vacant as though Rick had given up the fight and detached himself from his body. The doctor's explanation this morning loomed oppressively with gray shadows devoid of hope for her son's survival. Cold anguish raged through her bones with sharp stabs of horror. She felt trapped in numb reality. It pulled her about as though someone else was mechanically moving her arms and legs. She wanted to lay down beside her son and fall asleep permanently leaving behind this world with so much pain and suffering.

"Mrs. Tess," the doctor gently urged her. "You do understand it is the machine keeping your son breathing at this point. There is no brain activity, and his kidneys and liver have failed.

"Once we unhook the machine, it will only be a matter of minutes before we lose him. Would you like to leave the room before that time?"

Engulfed in a sea of darkness with eyes glued on her son, Marsha opened her mouth, but the words stuck in her tightened throat. She automatically drew close to her son pressing her face softly against his cheek. She smoothed his hair back from his forehead. She tenderly kissed him then turned Rick's head slightly. Taking a pair of scissors lying on the table, she carefully cut a piece of his flowing hair.

She paused and breathed heavily. Her voice dropped with exhaustion. "I'll say good-bye to him now, doctor."

Lowering her lashes, she clutched her fist tightly around the piece of her son's hair she held in her hand. She moved away awkwardly with her mouth twitching in bitter grief. Then she quietly left the room locked in anger and agony trying to make sense of it all.

AUSTIN 1992

Anne's lips curved in a slight smile. Her dark eyes challenged her husband. Blatant sexuality did not reflect her personality. Instead, she stood before him like a subtly seductive porcelain doll. The delicate features of her face invited him into her arms. He placed his fingers beneath her chin and lifted her face to his. Her head fell back revealing her soft slim neck, rose pedal lips, and pink cheekbones highlighting her dark lashes and eager eyes.

Her mouth softly parted when he touched her lips with his fingertips. Gently he traced her lips, then bent his tall frame to meet them. "I love you, Anne," he breathed softly brushing his mouth against hers.

He clutched her upward and guided her toward the bed. Her legs gripped around his waist, and her back arched to meet his flesh. His lips moved down gently caressing the sides of her neck then eagerly enfolded her mouth.

He felt her soft willing flesh beneath his touch. He closed his eyes savoring the warmth of her smooth hands fingering the muscles in his back. Pleasure gushed in his veins as her slender waist molded to his fingertips. Her legs gripped him. Fierce, jolting waves of pleasure shuddered through her body.

A small groan escaped her lips. Her body jerked towards his delighting in the urgency of his precise strong hands. Engulfed in the passion of his sensuous fingers tracing her skin with long strokes, wild sensations raced through her body. He watched her trembling thighs move further apart as his powerful legs pressed against them. He felt her arms pull him into her. Their bodies pressed together in unison with hungry bolts of excitement then shuddered in an explosion of fulfillment.

"Anne, you're beautiful," he breathed. She nestled her cheek against his warm skin. He playfully flickered his tongue on her sleek abdomen and traced his way up to her pulsing lips.

"You're beautiful too, sweetheart," she smiled when he enfolded her in his strong arms. She felt the warmth of the soft texture of his skin under her fingers. Then she glided them through his thick, silky hair. The corners of her lips smiled with contentment and exhausted exhilaration. She laid drowsily content in Derek's arms until they drifted off to sleep.

She woke up the next morning to the fragrance of eggs sizzling in the campfire and the thick spicy aroma of the surrounding pine trees. She stuck her head out of the trailer smiling widely at her husband preparing a scrumptious breakfast for the two of them.

"Well hello morning glory," Derek grinned.
She glanced at a tea bag already seeping in her cup.

"Isn't this nice. I can't think of a better way to wake up in the morning," she smiled. "I'm glad we had a chance to come up to the mountains and relax. You know, when I take the time to breathe in the beauty of nature, I know there really is a God.

"We've been in some beautiful hotels with luxurious accommodations, but I don't think I've ever seen a hotel with this much beauty and peace—not that I don't love being pampered once in awhile with the Jacuzzis, saunas and fine dining offered in the nicer hotels," she added with a smile. "Do you remember the two-story suite we rented in Colorado for a week with the jacuzzi right in the room? Now *that* I'd like to do again sometime."

"Yes, so would I, but you're right. I love being out here in the pines away from the heat of the city and the hustle and bustle of our regular routines. It's like we put a hold on reality for a short time and bask in simple leisurely pleasure. I think it's the peace of mind and smell of the pine trees I enjoy the most," he said, inhaling the scent.

"I agree. Time seems to fly by so quickly. In the day we're so busy exploring the mountain with the dogs, we hardly get back to the camp before night settles in. By the time we start a fire and cook dinner the stars are beginning to shine.

"I enjoy being able to sit down with you and talk with no interruptions. It's just you, me, the dogs, and the stars. I feel serene. It seems we rekindle a comfortable closeness in our relationship and our ability to communicate our thoughts with one another."

"It's great, isn't it? My parents took me all over the States with our trailer. I saw Niagara Falls, Mount Rushmore, Oregon, Big Sur, Old Faithful, and so many other places I'd like to take you, Anne."

"My childhood was so different. I went to New Jersey once with my sister. Then I lived in California for a short time, but I didn't get to travel and see things like you did. We were too busy struggling just to make ends meet. I hope you know how fortunate you were."

"I do. My parents were great—especially my mom. She never said an unkind word about anyone, and she was always smiling and singing.

"She belonged to the Sweet Adelaides. It a woman's

version of a Barbershop Quartet. She wrote beautiful poetry, and she was a great cook. We even had our own garden, and she canned fresh fruit and vegetables. I can remember my sister and I helping Mom every Christmas to make cut-out cookies and decorate each one. When I watch you bake, you remind me of her. I wish you could have met her, Anne. It's hard to believe she's been dead for ten years now."

"I wish I could have met her too. Do you think she would have liked me? I'm not as sweet and gentle as she was."

"She would have loved you, Anne. I know she would have."

"Well, Derek, she is still living in you. You have her talent and gift of music. Your soft side comes from her too. You got your sense of humor and your good looks from your dad though," she winked.

Anne and Derek reminisced, laughed, and shared their dreams through the week. The week did fly by quickly. Before they knew it, they were settled back into their routines in Austin.

A few weeks later the phone abruptly woke them. Anne glanced at the clock wondering who would be calling her so early.

"Hello, Anne. This is Gari-Sue. Listen, I ran across someone who will be in the San Francisco area and is willing to do a search for your son. Why don't you give it some thought and call me back if you're interested."

"Call you back! I don't need to call you back. Of course I'm interested. Just give me the details."

"He's going to be in the San Francisco area this week and could do the search then. How soon can you have the money?"

"I'll run to the bank now and have it over to you within an hour." Anne's hands trembled as she hung up the phone. She bolted out of bed to quickly throw on some clothes and get the money. She explained hurriedly to Derek while she dressed what was going on.

The next few days were filled with excited anticipation and an exhilaration Anne had never before felt. She stayed home close to the phone waiting anxiously for the call. On the third day, Anne rushed to the ringing phone hardly able to contain her excitement.

"Anne, do you have a pencil and paper?"

"Yes, I do," she stammered.

Gari-Sue gave Anne the information on her son and wished her luck.

Anne hung the phone up staring at the paper in disbelief. How could someone find her son so quickly when she had been unsuccessful for over a year? She shook her head determined to put aside her questions—grateful for the information before her. Anne turned to Vanessa. They both swung around dancing in each other's arms laughing and crying simultaneously.

"Mom, are you going to call right now?"

"I'm going to call Derek first. I don't know exactly what to say when I call. I hope he wants to see me. I hope his parents will let him see me."

She dialed the phone. Excitedly she informed Derek she had found her son and asked for his advice.

"Anne, I think you should take some time to collect your thoughts and calm down. Why don't you write what you want to say on a piece of paper first."

"That's a good idea, Derek, but I'm going to call today. I can't wait another day." Her heart continued to pound rapidly with excited exhilaration surging through her body.

Anne and Vanessa wrote out how she should start the conversation. She felt it was important to say who she was. She needed to give credibility to her claim by giving some background information on herself. She also wanted to suggest they call the social service agency. Then they could check the waiver of confidentiality she had placed with them. That would verify she, in fact, was the real birth mother.

Anne picked up the phone shaking with excitement and fear. She dialed the number but disappointedly received an answering machine message. I don't believe it, she thought, feeling her insides shake and her jaw tighten. "Of all times to get an answering machine," she mumbled. "My nerves can't take this." She decidedly hung up without leaving a message.

"I can't leave this kind of a message on an answering machine," she exasperatingly said to Vanessa. "I'll have to try back later."

"Mom, it's all right. This will give you a little time to calm down. I'm sorry, Mom, I hate to leave you like this, but I've got to go now. I won't be able to come back till late tonight. I wanted to be here when you called, but I know you'll want to try again early this evening. You can tell me all about it when I get home...I'm happy for you, Mom. Good luck."

Before Vanessa left the house she turned to her mother. "Mom, please don't get your hopes up too high. Derek is right. You need to take this time *to calm yourself down*. All right?"

Vanessa worried about Anne. Since her ordeal with Jeremy, Anne didn't take stress well. Vanessa didn't want Anne to get sick if things didn't turn out the way she had hoped.

"I don't think it's possible for me to calm down, Vanessa, but I'll try." Vanessa smiled with encouragement but still felt nervous about the outcome of her mother's search. Something didn't feel right to her.

"I love you, Mom. I'll see you later."

"I love you too, honey," Anne called out before Vanessa closed the door."

During the next three hours Anne called Maggie and Nina to tell them the good news. Then she rehearsed what she was going to say and waited in nervous anticipation. What if he doesn't want to have anything to do with me? What if the parents are resistant to me and angry with me for finding them? Am I strong enough to stand up to them? Am I strong enough to take the rejection if he hates me? What if he has some kind of a psychotic violent personality and wants revenge?

I have to do this. I've come too far to back down now. I have to do this for him. I owe him at least this much.

How am I going to tell other people about my son? What will they think of me? I don't know how I can face all of this. I'll have to deal with all of that later, she thought trying to control her nerves.

Anne waited for Derek to come home. The hours dragged by with exhausting anticipation. The moment Derek walked in, she dialed the number again. This time a woman answered the phone.

Anne froze for a minute, then found her voice.

"Hello. Is this Marsha Tess?"

"Yes, it is. Who is this?"

"Mrs. Tess, my name is Anne Blake. I gave birth to a boy on May 28, 1971 in San Francisco. I gave him up for adoption, and I believe you are the parents who adopted him." Anne listed some verifying information and gave Marsha the name of the social service agency to call for further verification.

Marsha, stunned by the irony and the incredible timing of this call felt a little apprehensive about the validity of this woman's claim. She slowly told Anne how much she loved Rick. She repeated how much he meant to her and that she did all she could do for him. She felt overcome with grief that this call didn't come a few weeks earlier if this was truly his birth mother.

"I intend to check with the social service agency to make sure you are who you say you are, and that this isn't some cruel joke." She hesitated. She then awkwardly blurted, "I don't know how to tell you this. I'm sorry. I...I lost him five weeks ago."

Anne went on with the conversation ignoring what Marsha had just said. It was as though she didn't hear it.

"Did you hear what I said? I lost him," Marsha breathed in a soft tremble.

"What do you mean you lost him? I don't understand. Did he run away from home?"

"It's a long story, one I will share with you in more detail after I verify your identity. He died five weeks ago as a result of a bronchial infection that settled in his lungs. A slight bronchial infection continually became more chronic as a direct result of the drugs he was taking."

Anne sat there speechless. Marsha's words burned like fire against her skin. Horror leaped into her limbs. Then, panic rose in her voice as she found herself sobbing and crumpled on the floor. Derek rushed over to her and stroked her shaking hand. From hearing part of the conversation and seeing Anne's reaction, he was able to decipher what had happened. He looked compassionately at her tiny face charged with grief, her pale quivering lips and her crumpled body. A shadow of shame and panic engulfed her with guilt tugging at her soul. He was afraid Anne might never recover from this.

Anne and Marsha exchanged passionate words of regret and sadness and some details about her son. Then Marsha agreed to call Anne back the next day with more details after she verified her identity.

Marsha and Anne talked several times over the next week. Marsha sent Anne a picture of Rick and a copy of his funeral service. Anne's mouth dropped in awe as she gazed at the picture staring at her. Richard was the likeness of Jay Pantonne with undertones of herself in her youth. This picture erased all doubt that somehow there had been a gross mistake and this was not her child. She couldn't pry her eyes off of her son's handsome face. She traced the picture with her fingers outlining every feature on his face. She examined every detail trying to picture his smile. She longed for just one chance to be able to see her son alive.

Her heart burned with the realization that she would never be able to hear him laugh, or see his beautiful brown eyes light up with his smile. She would never be able to hold him. Her skin crawled.

Anne decided she needed to formally acknowledge her son. She needed to put him to rest. She felt compelled to express her feelings of love and give tribute to the child she had denied for so many years. She prepared a Memorial service for him.

She planned to read the letter she had written to Richard long ago explaining the circumstances of his birth and relinquishment. She also planned to read the letter she wrote him after she discovered his death.

She carefully chose songs to reflect her sorrow and her

belief in the Lord. She tried to fight back her anger that she did not find him in time. How on earth could any reason possibly justify her son dying before they could meet—before she could touch his face. Why did he have to die not knowing she loved him? She hoped her faith and her family were strong enough to sustain her through this tragic time. Once again, peace seemed like an obscure impossibility.

Derek took Anne's hand as they walked into the church. He sat beside Vanessa. Anne went to the front of the church to begin the Memorial service.

She took a deep breath. Before heartache poured onto her cheeks, she lowered and fixed her eyes on the Eulogy paper before her. She scanned the faces of her friends and family seated before her. She drew strength from her husband's gentle blue eyes then rested on Vanessa's compassionate steady gaze.

Her eyes drifted to Nina's chalk-white face and her brother's firm, tightened jaw. The words trembling from her lips reflected the fundamental agony of her childhood and brimmed with pathetic excuses of her actions. Vague recollections of the past she so tightly kept closed in a secret part of her started to gush forth with amazing, sickening clarity.

Memories of Evan, Jay Pantonne, her pregnancy, and the events that lead to this moment swept through her mind as she struggled through the letter to her son. Anne's mind then snapped back to the present. She paused to wipe away her tears and plodded on to continue the Eulogy.

"I also would like to read the letter I wrote to Richard after I discovered he was gone.

Dear Richard:

I envisioned many scenarios about how it would be when I found you, but I never envisioned this. I found you—my son! I had three hours of ecstasy. I cannot describe the excitement of my anticipation of being with you.

When I reached your mother, she informed me I was five weeks too late. Your mother was and is a remarkable woman. I thank God you were sent to her. The tears and pain raging in her soft voice when she told me she lost you were filled with the love she felt for you. In a subsequent conversation this compassionate, kind woman told me in the midst of all her grieving and heart break that she was sorry I had to experience the pain of losing you twice.

Again, I thank the Lord for sending you to such a warm, caring woman. I pray for God's loving arms to wrap around her and heal her wounds and to soothe her pain—to give her comfort, guidance and strength. I pray my torment of finding you too late will subside. I pray for my family and Marsha's family for healing in this time of grief and loss.

I pray for understanding and forgiveness. I pray for peace and joy for you, Richard, as this time on earth seemed to be an exhausting struggle from the day you were conceived. You struggled so hard to survive your traumatic birth, rejection and alienation from your birth mother. You then seemed to be able to transfer your love and your life to a wonderful family. I'm sure there was much laughter and many warm and happy times. It seems, however, you struggled in your adolescence and early adult life with many things—and most of all with your ultimate enemy—drugs. I pray for the salvation of your soul and that you find everlasting peace in heaven.

I had such high hopes of a reunion in this lifetime, but now I know that will never happen. Richard, I pray some day we can still reunite in heaven. I hope God will bring us together in peace and love.

Anne played the song "Tears in Heaven." She wondered if her son would know her if he saw her in heaven. Time certainly did break her heart and bring her to her knees. She hoped there really was peace and truth beyond that door to eternity. Right now, she hoped to hold onto God's truth in grace.

Anne scanned the compassionate faces seated before her. Maggie sat near her aunt and uncle and a few friends from church. Her eyes reached out to Anne in compassion and love.

Leanne, refined and graceful as usual, sat with her husband and a few other friends from work. Her pixie haircut gave her a youthful vivacious look. Even today her eyes retained the sparkle and warmth Anne needed to see.

"I thank each one of you who is here with me today—not in judgment, but with comfort and understanding of my grief. What special people you are. You truly are fulfilling the prayer of Saint Francis.

"Lord make me an instrument of your peace. Where there is hatred...let me show peace. Where there is injury...pardon. Where there is doubt...faith. Where there is despair...hope. Where there is darkness...light.

"Where there is sadness...joy. O Divine Master, grant that I may not so much seek to be consoled as to console, to be understood as to understand, to be loved as to love. For it is in giving that we receive. It is in pardoning that we are pardoned. It is in dying that we are born to eternal life."

Anne lowered her head then took her seat between Derek and Vanessa. A warm wave of friendship and love crept up her spine and surrounded her weary spirit as her friends and family sang along with the songs she picked for the service. She plodded to her car numb with misery. The words of the last song rang in her ears.

Though the fig tree fail to blossom and no fruit be on the vine, and the field yield no food, I will praise Thee Lord divine.

Yet will I praise Thee—even in the night—even in the midst of a storm.

Chapter Eight

1993

Anne and Marsha struggled over the next year to come to terms with their son's death. They kept in touch with one another and met once in San Francisco shortly after the Memorial service.

One year later, Marsha completed a scrapbook of Rick's life to give to Anne. She drove to Austin for the Memorial Day weekend. Still struggling with many issues and working through her healing process, she was hesitant to open her fresh wounds. As the year passed, comfort and peace still eluded her. Yet, she found herself compelled to make the trip and meet with Anne.

This is one of the most difficult things I've ever done in my life, she thought. I must be crazy to put myself through this. I hope I'm doing the right thing. She gently stroked the photo album she painstakingly made. Rick would have wanted her to have this. I can't turn back now.

When Marsha drove up Anne's driveway, Anne ran to the door. She could hardly wait to see Marsha and the pictures she brought of her son's life. Anne, also struggling with her own issues, had taken a few months off teaching to work through her pain and to focus on healing. Although nervous with anticipation of Marsha's visit, she hoped it would help both of them in their grief. She knew her pain and Marsha's pain were very different, but felt their love and grief shared one common bond—their son. She felt overwhelmed with gratitude that Marsha would do this for her.

When she opened the door, all the barriers and misgivings about this trip crumbled. They embraced feeling the love they shared for Richard flow between them and feeling joined at the heart. Anne closed her eyes remembering Derek's soothing words. "Anne, the Bible tells us God forgave your sins before you were born.

"He already knew the depth of your sins, your thoughts, feelings, and even the number of your days on earth. Yet, he still chose to love you and all of us who believe in him.

"I believe we are all sent here to do a job and that each lesson we learn along the way brings us one step closer to completing our job. Once that job is completed, the Lord allows us to go home. You and I will never know what Rick's job was, but if you have faith and believe in the Lord, you know his job was completed, and he's now at peace."

Anne and Marsha tightly held onto one another. Anne could feel the warmth of her son flow through Marsha. Marsha could finally fit the missing puzzle piece of his past together for her son. They clung onto each other with support and compassion both happy for this time together. Yet, grief surged through them with its unrelenting grip. Both women painfully regretted that Rick couldn't be here to share this moment or the rest of their life's journey with them.

They smiled through their tears seeing Rick in each

other's eyes. They knew he would be more than just a faded memory. He would remain etched clearly in their souls with a never ending flame of love burning bright in their hearts.

Epilogue

"Closed" adoption can be the desire and in the best interest of all three parties in the triad. However, careful consideration should be placed on the permanent status "closed" adoption dictates. It severs the link between the birth parent and child prohibiting contact between them *forever*. The adoptee is a vital part of the triad. His choice and identity are lost when adoption records become permanently sealed, and his rights permanently severed.

Many organizations now support a choice of "Open" adoption in the adoption process. This allows the birth parent to communicate with the child in varying degrees established by all the parties in the adoption triad. The adoption movement urges awareness that the choice of "open" adoption can provide flexibility, honesty, personal comfort and choices within the triad. They feel "Open" adoption can greatly diminish many of the detrimental factors and negative life-long emotional torments of all the parties concerned.

Counseling is strongly advocated as both "Open" and "Closed" adoption each carry its own set of problems and concerns. The need to facilitate support and education to prospective adoptive parents and birth mothers is of strong concern in the adoption movement. Many locked in this system advocate counseling to birth parents to ensure their adoption decision is truly in the best interest of the child and the birth parents.

Information for the triad on different types of adoption choices and which type of adoption would best fit their needs should be available. It is essential to provide information to the birth mother of the variety of programs and assistance available to help keep her child should financial difficulty be a prime factor of relinquishment.

A societal shift in awareness and compassion is vital to acknowledge these problems and to set forth on a new level of reform.

References

This is a partial listing of informative books. If a book you find is not listed below, this in no way suggests that it is not an excellent resource.

Lifeline, The Action Guide to Adoption Search:
V. Klunder
Search—J. Askin, M. Davis
The ISC Searchbook—H. Gallagher, N. Sitterly,
P. Sander
Birthbond, Reunions Between BirthParents and Adoptees-What Happens After—J. Gediman, L. Brown
You Can Find Anyone—E. Fararo
(Adoption Family Awareness Center)
The Adoption Searchbook—Pure, Inc, Triadoption.

Search And Support Directory—Pure, Inc. Triadoption.
Search And Aftermath Adjustments—P. Sanders, N. Sitterly
Open Adoption: A Caring Option—J. W. Lindsay
The Whole Life Adoption—James Schooler
The Complete Adoption Handbook—K. Marshall Strom and D. Donnelly
I Would Have Searched Forever—Sandra K. Musser
The Other Mother—Carol Schaefer
Lost And Found—Betty Jean Lifton, Dial Press
How It Feels To Be Adopted—Jill Krementz,
Birthmark—Lorraine Dusky, M. Evans
The Adoption Triangle—Arthur Sorosky
Codependent No More—Melody Beattie
Troubled Teens, Troubled Parents—Pat Fullbright
Understanding And Avoiding Relapse—Paul Krippenstapel
Courage To Grieve—Judy Tatelbaum
On Death And Dying—Elizabeth Kubler-Ross
The Grief Process—David K. Switzer
Is There Life After Johnny?—Joy P. Gage
Lord, Heal My Hurts—Kay Arthur

Registeries:

ALMA
National Headquarters, Box 154,
Washington Bridge St., NY, NY 10033

INTERNATIONAL SOUNDEX
P.O. Box 2312, Carson City, Nevada 89702-2312

Newsletters:

PEOPLE SEARCHING NEWS
Box 22611 Ft. Lauderdale, FL 33335-2611

REUNIONS, THE MAGAZINE
P.O. Box 11727, Milwakee, WI 53211

Organizations:

ALARM: ADVOCACY LEGISLATION FOR ADOPTION REFORM
P.O. Box 6581, Ft. Myers, FL 33911

AMERICAN ADOPTION CONGRESS
1000 Connecticut Ave., N.W. Suite 9
Washington, D.C. 20036

AMERICANS FOR OPEN RECORDS
P.O. Box 401, Palm Desert, CA 92261

COUNCIL EQUAL RIGHTS ADOPTION
401 E. 74th Street #17D, NY, NY 10021

Most cities now have local chapters of search and support groups such as TRIAD and TRACERS. Check the yellow pages, local directory, and library.